ELEANOR

or

THE REJECTION
OF THE PROGRESS
OF LOVE

ALSO BY ANNA MOSCHOVAKIS

They and We Will Get into Trouble for This
You and Three Others Are Approaching a Lake
I Have Not Been Able to Get Through to Everyone

ELEANOR

or

THE REJECTION
OF THE PROGRESS
OF LOVE

Anna Moschovakis

COFFEE HOUSE PRESS
Minneapolis
2018

Coffee House Press books are available to the trade through our primary distributor, Consortium Book Sales & Distribution, cbsd.com or (800) 283-3572. For personal orders, catalogs, or other information, write to info@coffeehousepress.org.

Coffee House Press is a nonprofit literary publishing house. Support from private foundations, corporate giving programs, government programs, and generous individuals helps make the publication of our books possible. We gratefully acknowledge their support in detail in the back of this book.

LIBRARY OF CONGRESS CATALOGING-IN-PUBLICATION DATA

Names: Moschovakis, Anna, author.
Title: Eleanor, or, The Rejection of the Progress of Love /
    by Anna Moschovakis.
Description: Minneapolis : Coffee House Press, 2018.
Identifiers: LCCN 2017056242 | ISBN 9781566895088 (trade pbk.)
Classification: LCC PS3613.O7787 E43 2018 | DDC 813/.6—dc23
LC record available at https://lccn.loc.gov/2017056242

PRINTED IN THE UNITED STATES OF AMERICA
25 24 23 22 21 20 19 18   1 2 3 4 5 6 7 8

There is rupture and dissonance everywhere.
I am exhausted. I am.
—Vi Khi Nao, *Fish in Exile*

Obscured, the world's terrific
—Jane Gregory, *Yeah No*

Any thing may produce any thing.
—David Hume, *A Treatise of Human Nature*

ELEANOR

or

THE REJECTION
OF THE PROGRESS
OF LOVE

THE STORY SHE WAS READING was about a forty-three-year-old unarmed civilian shot to death in a Tampa Bay movie theater by a seventy-two-year-old retired police captain who'd become "agitated" by the man during previews. Eyewitnesses said the victim had been "texting loudly." Popcorn had been thrown.

She looked down from the screen at the bead of blood on her thumb. She watched it form a rivulet that ran down her palm and onto the white down comforter her friend had laid out on the bed for a Ukrainian folk singer arriving that night to teach a workshop in bilij holos at a nearby club. The blood formed a spot, brighter than the bead itself.

"He was a good, genuine person," it was said of the deceased. "He was just a funny guy. He brought life into every room." "Fate brought these two people together—it was ridiculous."

None of the witnesses tried to stop the altercation. The movie was about Navy SEALS on a mission in Afghanistan. Its title was *Lone Survivor.*

She stared at the spot and then back at her thumb, where fresh blood coagulated. She thought again of the thing that had happened—that she had made happen, or at least not prevented from happening. The room had floor-to-ceiling windows overlooking the expressway, from which she could hear the variegated moan of afternoon traffic. She was having a hard time getting up.

Charles Cummings, a former Marine and Vietnam veteran who left the theater with the victim's blood on his clothes, said he was shocked and saddened by the incident, which took place on his sixty-eighth birthday.

"I can't believe anybody would bring a gun to a movie," said Cummings.

"I can't believe I got shot," said the victim before he died.

The recipient of the texts was the man's three-year-old daughter, according to the *Tampa Bay Times*.

She looked away from the screen and then back again. When she clicked on the surveillance footage, popcorn filled the foreground like snow.

I
SPRING

SHE GOT UP.

Through the hollow door typical of the city's new high-rises she could hear the voice of her friend, who had interrupted her work to make a call to someone or answer a call from someone and was emitting a satisfied murmur the content of which was as indecipherable as its tone was clear.

She put on her coat, exited the spare room that doubled as her occasional office, kissed her friend—still listening and murmuring—on the cheek, returned the friend's wink with a wave, and left. She was alone in the hallway and in the elevator: mirrored walls coated with gray construction dust. She examined her reflection during the quick descent, then emerged into an empty lobby with plate-glass walls still covered in butcher paper and blue painter's tape; at its far end, she pushed open the massive plate-glass door.

It was cold—not as cold as was usual for early March, but colder than it had been for the last several weeks. People were out walking, dressed for fall or else for spring, having adjusted once and not wanting to adjust again, and now they were shivering and pulling their fall or spring coats around them, tilting toward the wind. She clutched and tilted with the rest, watched her boots cross a system of circling debris and slipped into the first coffee shop she saw, an unfamiliar place with a sidewalk board outside: COFFEE HERE.

She closed her eyes, opened them. The room was dim and sheathed in wood. The floor was light wood, the walls were dark wood, the ceiling was wood from which ivory paint had been scraped; ivory gauze curtains hung before the reclaimed wood-framed windows, which encased, instead of glass, sheets of plywood. A row of small barnwood tables lined the long sidewall opposite the counter, and at four of the five tables sat young people, alone or in pairs, silently drinking from mugs and, with one exception, absorbed in their devices. At the fifth table, next to the exception—a man of fifty in a plaid work shirt—she sat. The woman to her left was watching a movie, hot-pink buds in her ears. A desert car chase crossed the miniature screen.

The thing that had happened—that she had caused to happen, or that she had not caused but merely not prevented from happening— was as common as losing a tooth, as falling. It had come to define her. But was it of any consequence at all?

On the screen, Thelma and Louise's convertible sped past rocks, dunes.

Time passed. She stood, removed her coat, draped it over the chair-back to hold her place, nodded to her unshaven temporary neighbor, and ordered a coffee. She took out her laptop and began surfing the internet in the ways she used to, which brought her momentarily closer to the thing that had happened. Time passed. She rose to find the bathroom, not more than a storeroom outfitted with slop sink, toilet, and a wall coated in chalkboard paint on which was printed EMPLOYEES WASH HANDS.

Back at her table, the feeling of closeness to a time before—the familiar melancholy that came from surfing the internet in the ways she used to—had receded and been replaced by the new feeling, the one she struggled to describe.

The new feeling: a flesh-eating virus expanding its appetite beneath the skin.

Or, the new feeling: a helixed grating, eternal return.

Thelma: "Something has crossed over in me. I can't go back."

She checked the headlines. She read about a political prisoner in Cuba who had died at the end of a months-long hunger strike protesting a twenty-year sentence for an alleged infraction the details of which were hidden behind the *Times*'s paywall. She signed into her email, scrolled up and down her in-box, signed out.

She put on her coat, then thought better about leaving without revisiting the makeshift bathroom. When she returned, her neighbor was nodding over his mug; her laptop, which she'd left shut on her table, was gone.

Her reaction to sudden misfortune was programmatic: disbelief, followed by outrage, followed by self-abnegation. But unlike the stages of grief, which are said to progress toward acceptance, her pattern instead folded back on itself: disbelief, outrage, self-abnegation, outrage over the self-abnegation, disbelief at the outrage over the self-abnegation, etc.

She approached the counter and said something to the effect of My laptop's gone, did you see anything? The barista, staring at a phone through clear plastic–rim glasses, said something about Angelopoulos (which she pronounced with a hard "g") having been run down by a motorcycle; this comment was directed over the barista's shoulder, presumably to someone in the shallow, semi-hidden kitchen.

She felt a shift in her guts—subcutaneous creature—at the transition from disbelief to outrage. She repeated something about the laptop while pointing to her table, which she now saw was hidden by the tall back of her vacant chair. The café had become crowded, raucous: 3:35. School was out. A swarm of tweens and teens.

The barista winced in an approximation of sympathy and said something about a police station, gesturing around the corner to the right. Her pale arm was tattooed with a diagram of some kind of electronic circuit; at one edge of the circuit was a badly covered heart.

Nodding to the barista, she gathered her things and left, pausing for two teens to finish fake-wrestling between her body and the door.

She knew exactly how it would go. She would walk down Fourth Avenue toward Flatbush, past the silent army of men wiping down SUVs at the Golden Touch; past PL$ Check Cashing, empty as usual; past the tiny Oaxacan taco place and the overpriced organic bodega, replaying the last half hour in her head. She would berate herself in all the usual ways—over the problem of her relationship to techno-convenience and capitalism, her problem with focus, with priorities, with time. The wind would lacerate through her too-thin coat. It would feel good.

Eventually she would turn up Bergen Street, quieter and comparatively sheltered from the wind, and she would have sunk into the abandon of self-abnegation, which would allow her to notice things of beauty but always despite herself, so that the striped awnings of the corner deli would be beautiful despite herself, the sound of conversation caught through an opening door would be beautiful despite herself, and despite herself she would notice how her body moved the way she wanted it to, how she was neither obese nor undernourished, how she was breathing on her own and not with some machine or the help of an inhaler, how she was more autonomous than most and still not halfway to death (according to statistics, and what else could she go by?), and how despite herself there was something good, something awful and good about being alive.

By the time she crossed Underhill she would be thinking about her lover, hoping he'd be home when she arrived at his door, knowing that she would enter the apartment and look for him in whatever corner he was hiding, reading, a dark T-shirt draped over his arced back, smoking; and that she would take his cigarette from his hand and extinguish it, then remove his shirt and kneel clumsily beside him, lean around his chest while he unbuckled his belt; that she would tug down his jeans and that despite herself, she would feel a generosity toward this man, toward his beauty and the beauty of all of his parts—of the Texas-shaped birthmark next to his navel and the pink light from the window illuminating Texas—and that after taking in all of this various beauty she would take certain of his parts into her mouth, and that this act would eclipse the events of the afternoon, the lingering response to the thing that had happened and the acute response to the theft by some kid of her laptop; that it would eclipse her feeling of specific culpability for these things and of vague culpability for the other things (the Cuban prisoner, the Tampa Bay gunman and the dead Greek auteur); that there would then be nothing left but the parts and their beauty and the pink light and its beauty and the awful and good sound of her lover's breathing and then, for a moment, not.

After he'd gotten up to shower, she would take her Doc Johnson Pocket Rocket from her bag, turn it on and press it against the crotch of her jeans, close her eyes, and imagine a room full of tattooed baristas and fake-wrestling teenagers, none of them paying any attention to her at all.

Halfway down the block of her lover's apartment, she was reaching into her bag to feel for her keys. She pulled them out and held them in her fist like a weapon while the top edges of the canvas book bag, too empty with the laptop gone, flapped in the wind.

Her name is Eleanor. Did you think she didn't have a name?

OR DO I MEAN that it had come to *create* her? Things don't necessarily happen in order.

By the time the critic offered to read my manuscript, our interactions had progressed from a logistical email exchange about a photo shoot at his apartment for the magazine where I work to a late-night three-hour session at a bar, followed by a volley of text messages in which logistics played no part. Since he has a reputation for being careful with his time and, I believed, would not ask twice (once in person while admittedly drunk on whiskey, but then again in a clear-eyed morning email) to look at something unless he meant it, I sent him the file.

While waiting to hear back, I couldn't work on the book. I turned to other, mostly mundane, commitments I'd been neglecting, my process of revision reduced to a sequence of emails (subject: novel) typed to myself from work or on my phone while walking.

I typed, "the erotics of conversation"—which autocorrected to "the erotica of conversation"—and determined this belonged in the scene between Eleanor and the Frenchman in part 3.

I typed, "this is about numbness not about toys / no toys."

I typed, "the continuity of identity after a rupture," which was a direct quote from the critic's initial response, at the bar, to my attempt to describe my book's "plot." I left the notes in my in-box where they were quickly buried beneath incoming requests and reminders of things owed.

There was a backstory to my interest in the critic, but only I knew it. His recent high dive from theory into practice had resulted in a Caméra d'Or–winning film, *Audience,* for which he'd spun five minutes of Hi8 footage from a youthful encounter with Samuel Beckett on his deathbed into an extended meditation on theater, failure, and the anxiety of influence. Though he was raised mostly in England he was an Irish national; the win was a first for that country, the attention copious and laudatory. In an interview for *T Magazine,* below a photo of him dressed in Lagerfeld at the White Horse Tavern, the critic was quoted saying the film had "made itself," a claim I thought crumbled under scrutiny. His film was built like a Lego tower—wild but sturdy, its connections airtight. The pressure points, he explained to me over our first drink together, came not from his telling of the encounter itself but from the way the film troubles the gap between what's desired and what's delivered in a story, a troubling he termed—dramatically—*the wreck.*

Some of this phrasing was familiar to me. Nearly twenty years earlier, when he was a graduate student and I a part-time undergrad, I had taken his survey course in twentieth-century drama theory, "Artaud, Beckett, Brecht." I was diligent. I wrote in my notebook: *pressure.* I wrote *delivered ≤ wreck.* I never raised my hand.

Now, the critic's comments on my still-fragile manuscript—both in person at the first bar and in subsequent bars and also in the margins of the document itself—would call for greater and more specified points of pressure; "pressure" became the paradigm of the radiating diagram I composed over the course of an afternoon, after two pots of coffee, on a sheet of fresh graph paper when beginning the new revision. "Pressure" was represented by arrows between two or more terms circled with ballpoint pen.

I wasn't interested in replicating the critic's formula on the page. But I knew that my novel—if that's what it was—needed help. It had begun to seem like a sequence of nested clauses, an interminable sentence requiring too many readings to locate the verb. The task of the revision, which I hoped would be my last, was to remedy this defect without bending, submissively, to the critic's significant will.

In place of Legos, I imagined a Jenga tower, one move before collapse.

Or: one move before the expectation of collapse.

HER LOVER, TOO, has a name. It's Abraham.

They sat against the southwest-facing wall of Abraham's corner apartment, sharing a smoke. He wore a beige towel wrapped around his waist; the skin on his shoulders and chest was still moist, like condensation on a glass. Eleanor's boots and sweater lay beside her on the floor. The radiator clucked, emitting an unnecessary amount of heat. The sun was gone, the sky a glowing field partitioned by buildings.

"Skybluepink," murmured Eleanor.

"Huh?" Abraham took a drag.

She was deep in self-abnegation now. She let it fill her while the cigarette was extinguished, another rolled and lit.

"Did you hear about Angelopoulos?" Eleanor asked.

"Who?"

"Remember the movie with Lenin's head floating down the river?"

"Uh-huh."

"He was hit by a motorcycle in Athens."

In clement weather, Abraham rode a motorcycle.

"Was he riding?"

"Walking."

"Oh."

Abraham got up, stretched his arms over his head, his dance training evident in their form. Winter had turned his olive skin wan. The towel fell from his waist and he bent to retrieve it from the parquet floor.

"Did he die?"

Eleanor nodded.

He pulled the towel back around himself, tucked in the ends. A string dangled from the bottom edge where the terry cloth had frayed.

"Happens."

Abraham's relationship to death, to talking about death, was unlike Eleanor's. Abraham talked about death as if it were something that happened every day, while Eleanor—fully knowing that it does happen every day, every second, more frequently than that—still spoke of death as if it were remarkable, imbued with import. Especially when there was something improbable about its delivery.

"Like Barthes and the laundry truck."

Silence.

"Frank O'Hara and the dune buggy."

"Who?"

The lack of shared references between herself and her lover was, Eleanor mostly believed, a key ingredient of their dynamic, was what enabled their continued erotic connection amid a seeming drought of eros in the relationships of people they knew. She also interpreted certain elements of his personality—this relation to death, for instance, an embodiment of Sein-zum-Tode—as living examples of things she'd read about in the very books that distinguished her intellectual territory from his.

She stood up, walked over to her lover, put her arms around his neck, and kissed him.

"So, something happened. So someone stole my laptop, and I can't think yet of what I might have lost."

She had realized immediately what she'd lost. But she wasn't ready to think about what the loss might mean. Abraham kept his plans to meet a friend for drinks, and Eleanor stayed in to sit on his futon and watch something on his computer. There was a small stack of kung fu movies and dance documentaries she wasn't in the mood for. She streamed *Tropic Thunder* and laughed until she cried. Then she put in *Pina* and watched the first twenty minutes, which ends with three dancers, two men and a woman, repeating a series of moves on a stage set suggestive of a café. First one of the men, in the role of director, entwines the limbs of the other two dancers and guides them through their choreography until they've learned it. Then he leaves them to perform.

The woman flings herself limply into the man's waiting arms, which extend, bent at the elbow, from his waist like a shelf. She falls: the man is pure passivity. She scrambles to her feet. They repeat the sequence dozens of times, increasing the tempo with each round. She flings, falls, regroups, tries again. She flings, falls, regroups, each attempt more frantic but no less determined than the last.

Examining the dancers' faces, Eleanor was struck by the difference between them. The stress of the imperative of self-restraint—not to react, not to prevent a fall—is unmistakable in the features of the man, while the expression of the woman, the one who will go home bruised, is open.

She ejected *Pina* and streamed *My Dinner with Andre,* and then she went to sleep. Wallace Shawn lay in bed next to her, fully clothed, on top of the covers. He spoke to her as if she were Andre Gregory, as if the film had slid effortlessly from the computer screen onto Abraham's bed.

"And I mean, I just don't know how anybody could enjoy anything more than I enjoy reading Charlton Heston's autobiography, or, you know, getting up in the morning and having the cup of cold coffee that's been waiting for me all night, still there for me to drink in the morning!" said Wallace Shawn.

"And no cockroach or fly has died in it overnight. I mean, I'm just so thrilled when I get up and I see that coffee there just the way I wanted it, I mean, I just can't imagine how anybody could enjoy something else any more than that! I mean . . . I mean, obviously, if the cockroach—if there is a dead cockroach in it, well, then I just have a feeling of disappointment, and I'm sad."

Eleanor looked at Wallace Shawn when he said this, but he continued to stare at the ceiling.

"But I mean, I just don't think I feel the need for anything more than all this."

"But Mr. Shawn," she said after pausing to work up the nerve, "you haven't answered my question. My question is not about disappointment per se. My question is not about sadness. My question—"

Wallace Shawn turned to face Eleanor with a look of unadulterated tenderness. She began to whisper:

"When a person doesn't catch another person but it's a planned not-catching, it's a choreographed not-catching, and the not-caught person gets bruised as a result, how are we supposed to feel? Have you followed the discourse on sadomasochism since the '80s, since we were told we can't play with power, that nobody can? I'm confused about power, Wally—can I call you Wally? I'm confused about roles and the edges of roles. My question is not about the pleasure of the coffee or the disappointment of the cockroach. My question"—and here her whisper became nearly inaudible—"is about the bruise—"

In the morning, Wallace Shawn was gone. Eleanor was on her side, one wrist hanging off the bed. Abraham lay behind her, the fronts of his knees tucked into the backs of hers, his arm around her torso as if to hold her up.

"THERE'S SOMETHING ON MY MIND that I need to tell somebody. I don't think I can talk to anyone who's already invested in my life. Can I tell you this thing?" The critic's eyes shone as we started in on drink number four.

He has a name—it's Aidan—but he was still the critic to me.

We had met in broad daylight, though it was overcast, to discuss the comments he'd sent about my manuscript, first taking in an exhibit at a museum downtown, a retrospective of a performance artist in whom we were both only mildly interested except for some of his early works, which were underrepresented in the show. The bar we'd wandered into was a neighborhood fixture, virtually unchanged since the 1990s, with smoke-stained walls and plastic covers on its brocade couches and chairs; the critic and I sat across from each other, a tabletop Ms. Pac-Man between us. He took off his glasses—his face transformed, I had to adjust—and set them on the game's screen. We drank three whiskeys each in quick succession, attempting small talk until the alcohol took effect.

By the time the conversation turned to my book, the first question he had was about the function of Eleanor's lover in the story. It was clear from the start that the critic was under the assumption— and perhaps this should not have surprised me; he'd just made a personal film—that in essential ways I was Eleanor and Eleanor was me. He had been suspicious, in our first conversation before I'd sent him my draft, even of the fact that I'd chosen to write in the third person, but then—in the manner of people who think like the critic—he theorized the choice by suggesting that a character who's lost her data has lost her "I." Still, he was bothered by a sense that the lover was tossed in out of some obligation to my "real life"— about which, to be clear, he knew nothing.

(I had experimented, after reading his comments, with removing the lover completely, which entailed among other things losing several scenes in which sex acts were described. But my decision to include these in the first place was made deliberately, in response to a sense—which I didn't share with the critic now, too embarrassed to bring it up in person while still absorbing his candid marginal responses to my portrayal of said acts—that depictions of sex and sexual dynamics in novels, especially heterodynamics, especially in novels by women, tend to invite a particular kind of reductive critique, or else sensationalism when such dynamics happen to be central to a book. For reasons that remained obscure to me, I had an urge to face this vulnerability—to some extent, at least—rather than defend against it by writing a novel in which nobody fucks.)

When speaking of literature, even of my flawed draft, the critic was one of those men—every example that comes to mind is a man— who speak only in subordinated sentences, developed theories: he would part his lips (his accent underscored the effect) and whatever insight emerged was of an apparent authority and completion that I knew from experience I could muster only after substantial thought, the painful suppression of doubt, and rehearsal before a mirror.

But on other subjects, he was capable of a frankness and spontaneity that saved our conversation from becoming a one-sided drill. We talked about our diagnosed and undiagnosed disorders and about a shared obsession with psychological self-tests—*I feel sad / I feel discouraged about the future / All of the time / Good part of the time*—some of which I'd been both imitating and incorporating wholesale into my writing, though I was uncertain about how much of that material to let stand in the book because of what seemed to have become a minor literary zeitgeist. We sparred tentatively about politics and gossiped freely about the few people we knew in common, using the act of gossiping less for its prurient pleasures than for the pleasure of the alliance it establishes between participants.

My concern about the zeitgeist embarrassed me, and I returned to the subject to confess this to the critic. When he asked why, I cited my book's many unoriginal traits: its episodic structure, its banal story line tracing the alienation of the individual in late capitalism, and more. But what really embarrassed me was that I imagined a readership at all.

The music the bartender was playing was, like the décor, a fossil from when the bar was new and popular, when I went there frequently at the end of long nights waitressing and drinking, to drink more. Now, decades later, I felt no different; it was as if I were still inside my twenty-three-year-old body, as if I were listening with its ears to the caterwauling of Kristin Hersh and Mudhoney, looking with its eyes at the bartender's faded band T-shirt and slack posture; as if I were feeling in its chest the bliss of getting drunk in good company, that gradual dissolving of boundaries between the body and its setting. The critic, who had turned around to watch the bartender pop open a row of cans of Genesee, said something about how Meyerhold would take his actors to study the gestures of factory workers, and at that moment all of the sensory data— the feeling of the plastic covering on the chair cushion beneath me; the stillness of my slouched position, which belied the attention I was paying to the critic's every word; the awareness of an unskilled pool game playing out in the darkened back of the bar and of the weeknight procession past the windows behind me— became incoherent, scrambled, as if pointing in two directions at once. As this eruption of feeling tempered by thought was occurring, I stared weakly at the critic—it was the longest moment of silence we'd shared—and although he couldn't know the palimpsestic time warp I was in, he stared back with an attention that felt like company, and it was at that moment that our acquaintance began to feel something like friendship.

When he returned from the bar with the fourth round of whiskeys, the critic's demeanor had changed. He brought his hands together on the Ms. Pac-Man screen and began to rub his left fingers, one by one, with his right thumb. "Of course you can tell me," I said in response to his unexpected request. "You can tell me anything you want, because we are new friends and this is what new friends can do for each other." I don't know why I said that.

He stopped rubbing to sip from his glass.

"My dentist's daughter—my dentist and I are friendly, I've been seeing him for years—goes to an elite private school. And for this year's science fair, she wanted to take advantage of the art department's new 3-D printer. She devised a project"—he stopped to extract his scarf from under his coat on the chairback and drape it over his shoulders, as if whatever he was about to say would precipitate a drop in temperature in the room—"a project that has to do with genetic codes, sequencing. She's adopted and wanted to know more about her biological identity, so she got her code read at one of those online genome-mapping sites. They aren't allowed to interpret health-related results anymore, so she resorted to probability: she researched the diseases with the greatest impact on mortality in the parts of the world that showed up significantly in her code—a broad spread, from East Asia to southern Africa—then crunched the statistics and made an annotated model of the *death data,* as she called it, using the 3-D printer. This girl is in middle school, mind you."

He took a sip from his whiskey. Plastic squeaked as I shifted position in my chair. "She must be—"

He raised a finger to silence my interjection.

"So while I'm in the chair waiting for the novocaine to take effect, she's in the exam room distracting me with this description of her entry—which would go on to win first prize, of course—and when I got home that night, in a fever of sorts, I ordered one of the test kits myself. What I knew, but she didn't, was that although the company that provides the results won't fully interpret them because of liability, it's easy enough to find another company that will."

He stopped short and turned his head slightly to the left, like someone looking for something he doesn't expect to find. The indentation of a closed-up piercing was just visible on his earlobe. In the days of "Artaud, Beckett, Brecht" I'd thought he looked like Artaud (suspecting even that he cultivated the resemblance), but now I saw Wittgenstein as he was once shot in half-profile, with a far gaze, set jaw, and open-collared shirt just like the one the critic now wore beneath his scarf. I tried to figure out what was required of me in my capacity as new friend, but before I could say anything, he turned to face me and went on.

"That was weeks ago. The test came, but I haven't sent it in. I have—"

The music cut out and he looked momentarily confused. "I haven't been able to sleep. Two days ago I asked Laurance"—Laurance was the name of the critic's girlfriend, about whom I knew exactly what had been revealed in my magazine's fluff piece, which wasn't much—"to marry me, and she said she would love to *if it weren't for the ice cube in my heart.*"

I tried not to laugh; his face was ash.

"She's right, you know. And I got to wondering if maybe I really should do the test, if it might answer certain . . . questions, or *a* certain *question* . . . that has lingered."

At this point he set his head down on Ms. Pac-Man and left it there for a full minute at least.

"He used to do that, you know," he said after lifting it. The Breeders came on: "Cannonball."

"Who did?"

"Beckett. Just bow out for a moment. Not impolitely, according to reports."

I looked at him.

"So what is it?" I asked.

"What?"

"The . . . question?" I couldn't tell which one of us was being thick.

"Oh." He upended his glass and drained it. "Just the usual. Whether my grandfather was also my father."

There was nothing, at this point, that I could think to say, so I sat in silence, wearing what I hoped was an alert and kind expression as the critic told me how his mother had always refused to talk about her estranged father; how his dad's early death, a probable suicide, was never discussed or explained; how he himself had always suffered from hormone imbalance and a compromised immune system, two known risks of inbreeding (a word he pronounced with scare quotes). "Could you talk to your mother . . . ?" I asked tentatively. His head went down on the table again.

"What I don't know," he said when he raised it, "is whether it's kinder, whether it is righter"—here he coughed, suddenly shy—"to try to find out before Laurance makes her decision, or if . . ." His dilemma didn't seem to have a second branch, but I nodded encouragingly in case one would manifest. It didn't.

We sat in silence as I finished my drink. I felt unable or unwilling to offer advice, my instincts tempered by my clouded sense of his confession—his disclosure, presented as confession. The bar was empty now except for us and the pool players, and in the wake of the critic's narrative this lack of company, along with the fact that the music had stopped again, created an aura of intimacy for which we were unprepared. He was still doing the thing with his fingers, methodically rubbing one after the other—pinky, ring, middle, index, thumb—his palm turned to the ceiling. As soon as he finished with one hand he switched to the other: thumb, index, middle, ring, pinky. I wanted to place my hands on his, to make a gesture that might transmit the full weight of my sympathy. But our friendship was new, the question of physical contact unresolved.

He was going to be gone for three weeks on tour overseas—his film was appearing in festivals in several Scandinavian countries—and before parting, we stood outside the bar as it began to drizzle and waited for a smoker to come out. I bummed an American Spirit and we smoked it together, pressed against the building for shelter, and watched cars pass by on the shimmering asphalt. Without preface and without shifting his gaze from the street, the critic raised his free hand to my throat and palpated roughly on both sides of my esophagus.

"The thyroid gland is a butterfly-shaped organ composed of two wings connected by the isthmus," he said in the voice of a BBC announcer, then dropped his hand and flicked the cigarette to the curb.

On his way home he texted me a video of an inflated giraffe levitating outside a storefront, illuminated by streetlights, bowing gently in the rain.

PERHAPS IT WASN'T the case that she had caused the thing that had happened, or even that she'd allowed it. Perhaps the thing—the first thing, that is, which had come to define her, which was equal parts a happening and a not-happening—would have happened or not-happened no matter what she had done or said or felt, no matter how she had interpreted the words and events and emotions surrounding it.

Perhaps it was, as people sometimes say, "beyond her control."

She thought about control. That led her to think about religion, which led her to think about progress.

The previous morning, she'd picked up a book from Abraham's bathroom shelf while she was sitting on the toilet, a collection of essays—*The Idea of Progress Since the Renaissance*—that she'd bought for a dollar at the neighborhood used bookstore. The opening chapter's thesis—as far as she could tell from the pages she'd skimmed before Abraham's voice called her back to the morning, the coffee, the grapefruit and toast—was that Christianity and progress are inextricably entwined in the story of Western thought. This made sense to Eleanor; she was not a Christian, and she found the notion of progress alien. (She was less alienated by the notion of progression, though it too was not above suspicion. There were so many instances in which it wasn't clear if one thing preceded another or followed it, and whether the distinction mattered.)

She'd read: "The scholar in search of continuing themes in the history of Western civilization is confronted with two quite different types of material: patterns of action, on the one hand, and patterns of thought, on the other."

She'd read: "A thought is fully as much an event as a war, and thinking falls into observable patterns which, in turn, have histories of their own, no less a part of the ongoing life of humanity than the more conventional subject matter of historical research."

As she was flushing the toilet and washing her hands with the last drops of glycerin soap and examining her reflection in the dust-covered mirror, she had considered the difference between thinking and doing and the relation of that difference to the concept of progression. She'd considered how the thing that had happened had in a sense led her here, how it was in a sense the cause of her new circumstance; and how it was equally true that her new circumstance—this stack of books by the toilet, this drop of soap—was the cause of the thing, since the thinking about the thing from her current position and the thing itself were (also *in a sense*) the same. She had then returned to the morning, to Abraham and the grapefruit, and to a story on the radio about how laboratory scientists in Russia had succeeded in reproducing life derived from plant matter trapped in the Siberian permafrost for thirty thousand years. Since she'd tuned in midway through the story, she did not know what the scientists had expected to happen or the degree of their surprise, which made the discovery seem less eventful in both the thought-event way and the war-event way.

What is really beyond our control, she thought now, as she finished her breakfast (a banana this morning, cut up and topped with yogurt and granola) and got in the shower, and then as she washed her hair and decided not to shave her armpits and leaned around the plastic curtain to kiss Abraham, on his way to the studio in work pants with goggles on his head, good-bye—what is really beyond our, beyond anyone's, control is—and then she revised her thought out of existence, emerged from the shower, applied her usual oils and lotions, and stepped into her clothes and boots, pausing automatically at Abraham's computer to check email before walking out the door.

FROM: Danny K.M. <████████████@gmail.com>
TO: eleanornoteleanor@gmail.com

Hi there. I was just wondering if you have lost a macbook laptop recently. The reason why I am asking is that I am visiting a friend and he has this laptop full of your information, documents, photos, etc. It is very weird to me and I know how it feels when something of value gets stolen, especially the data. So please confirm if you have indeed lost a laptop or not or maybe you might have given it to my friend for keeps. he is not here right now and he wont for the next few days so I wanted to help you get your data back at least. I am a computer guy and know what i am doing and also I had my own mac. Please understand that I most likely wont be able to give you your laptop back because that would destroy the friendship between me and my friend but I could at least sneak you out all the data that you want.
Please, understand that I am trying to help you ok!
Respond urgently!

Eleanor knew that first responses should rarely be trusted. They might be made sense of, especially when they fit into a known taxonomy (outrage —» self-abnegation, etc., for example), but they should not be treated as maps or as blueprints; they should be treated, at best, as a sketch—a Rorschach test, the interpretation of which is more important than the thing itself.

This does not stop them from appearing as blueprints, or maps, with the potential to lead one irrevocably astray. Or in a worst-case scenario, to bring the building down.

It is very weird to me.
I know how it feels.
because that would destroy the friendship
Please, understand
Respond urgently!

She read the phrases until they lost their definitions, until they were reduced to strings of phonemes—all but a few of the words, which could not be reduced, which would not relinquish their associative and affective powers. These she studied—"feels," "friendship," "respond"—as she tried to construct or identify the appropriate reply to a gesture that seemed so full of ambivalence that even she, an adept, could not instinctually read it.

She paced the small apartment: ten steps to the front windows, eight steps to the interior sidewall, fifteen steps to the galley kitchen that led back to the minuscule bedroom. She crossed to the window that was farthest from the unnecessarily hot radiator and perched on its sill. She sweated. She thought about dogs, how they can't sweat, how none of the dogs she had ever known had sweated. She tried panting, having read somewhere that intentional hyperventilation can reset the human nervous system. She set the timer on her phone for one minute, but the panting nauseated her and made her violently thirsty, so after twenty seconds she returned to the kitchen and poured a glass of vodka over ice. She considered removing her boots and socks to cool down. She removed her boots and socks.

She considered the likelihood that this was a phishing scheme, that Danny K.M. was not a person but a front for an organized laptop-thieving ring. She made a cursory web search and dismissed this hypothesis. Danny K.M. was real, according to the evidence, as real as Eleanor herself. She felt something like relief, then something like annoyance at her relief, and then she let out her breath—she hadn't realized she was holding it—through flapping lips, in a burst, like a horse.

She drank, and then she called a friend and hung up on his voicemail. She drank more, then called another friend and hung up on their voicemail. She drank more, and then she decided to read her cards. She opened the dresser drawer that Abraham had cleared for her—not long ago but long enough ago that it had begun to resemble other drawers she'd had in other apartments belonging to other men—and took out her tarot deck, removing the scarf she'd been taught to wrap it in to repel negative energy, in which she didn't believe. She removed *Tarot for Your Self* from the drawer and set it beside her, then shuffled the cards and thought about her question.

As she shuffled, she did not think about the thing that had happened before (thing-prime), nor did she think about the other thing that had happened more recently—her lost data, thing #2—nor did she think about the email she had just received from Danny K.M. Her question was of a more general nature: "Who," she asked the cards, "am I in relation to these things?"

She turned a card, then opened the book and read.

17. The Star. Aquarius. *Tzaddi.*
Meditation. Inexhaustible inspiration. Spiritual regeneration. Using active imagination and visualization. Artistic and scientific inspiration. Formulating your ideals and goals. Examining your hopes for the future. Using systems of self-insight such as astrology, Tarot, numerology, etc.

At this point Eleanor paused and smiled. She continued:

Living by your own truth and values rather than those of the outer world. "Freedom is nothing left to lose." Altruism. Nonconformity. Doing the unexpected. The calm after the storm; release after imprisonment. Freedom.

At this point Eleanor's eyes began to glaze over. She skipped a few sentences.

Frankness. Disclosure or discovery of something. A desire to participate in the enlightenment and consciousness-raising of all humankind.

At this point a clammy sensation began to rise from Eleanor's palms and travel up her wrists and forearms. She considered getting up to take a cold shower, but the sensation passed, or rather merged with her overall feeling of discomfort, which she was by now accustomed to ignoring. She skipped to the end.

Being the "star," the center of attention. Public recognition. Being the leader and spokesperson for others. Stubbornly clinging to fixed ideas.

This time, the sensation would not subside. It moved up through her shoulders and chest and into her neck, where it pulsed near her lower jaw. It was the words *fixed ideas* that did this to her. She had once seen a documentary about an artist from New York who became a cannibal for a day while living in a quasi participant-observer relationship with a Peruvian tribe and had to contend forever after with the consequences of his actions.

The thing about consequences, Eleanor thought, is that they are a fiction. And fiction is real. And reality is consequential, but only when you let it be. Consequences, she thought, now speaking her thoughts to the room, "are like mud. You get stuck in them, and either you drown and die, or a dry spell comes to return the mud to dust, and you dig your way out." She looked out the window as she spoke, a little louder now, her speech swallowed by the sirens of a passing ambulance: "You just don't know. You never really know."

The thing that had happened—the first thing, thing-prime—had this kind of consequence, the mud kind. Eleanor began to feel something new take place inside her, the presence of something beneath her skin, at the core of her extension into space, running from top to bottom or from bottom to top—something fibrous, organic like sugarcane, or possibly of some high-tech material that had the quality of moisture and the quality of disintegration in equal measure. This material was pulling apart, or being pulled apart, as if by some weaver separating strands in order to dye them fresh colors and make them into something new. She felt the pulling apart—felt it as a novel but recognizable sensation—but she could not feel the hand of the weaver. It was as if there were no hand. Nothing working on her, nothing looking to improve or profit from her. There was nothing, nothing at all.

She finished her vodka and stood, inducing a moment of dizziness that somehow reoriented her to the present. She returned to the cards and the book and the section on The Star.

Sample Affirmation: My inner being shines like a star, guiding my actions, renewing and cleansing me.

She opened Abraham's computer, logged back in.

ABRAHAM PUT ON his goggles and [power saw, exhaust, plywood]

Eleanor typed.

Abraham [measuring tape, chop saw, dust]

Time passed.

Eleanor waited [window, street, trash, oily slick, tea]

Abraham broke for lunch [goggles, flirting, cigarette, sandwich, cigarettes, flirting, goggles]

Time passed.

Eleanor read:

> Hello Eleanor,
> Ok thanks for coming back so fast! I hope I can find enough DVD's to burn all your stuff! You have a massive amount of Data on the laptop. I am sorry to hear about your computer getting stolen. I hope that it was not my friend but someone else who may have sold it to him, regardless its a bad thing. I'll probably drop off the data at your work or send it via mail depending on what is more convenient. I just arrived from my home country

and I have to find my way around here. I wish i could just return the computer to you. That would be the best but again as you might imagine thats the least possible option unless, unless . . . I can convince him to give it back to you if you pay him. That is highly unlikely but i can play on his conscious and he might feel guilty and give it back!

Here is some info regarding your data. Your personal profile is about 42Gb, I am not sure how i can send you all that data unless I burn about 10 DVD, each about 4.3Gb, that might be the best option but like I said I just arrive in the country about two days ago and I have only about $50 on me and thats all I have until I get a job. Another option would be if you have an ftp site where I could download all the info which I bet would take days until is complete but its one way of doing things. Bad thing is that the harddrive is difficult to get too otherwise I would have done something but he will notice. If you have any other suggestion please let me know ok? We need to be done with everything before he comes back on Tuesday from L.A.!

Eleanor typed, waited. Time passed.

Abraham packed up [goggles, flirting, cigarette, bike]

Eleanor [vodka, tarot, tea]

Eleanor read:

You are right on the money of not buying back your computer. I was just wondering what your stance was on that considering, as you said, that computers are quite expensive. I'm glad some of the data is backed up at least. I'll drop the DVD off at your work.

Again I am sorry for what happened and on another note, the guy is not my friend at all actually. He just let me use "his" computer when he went to L.A. cause I need internet access! Have a good day!

Abraham rode [windlash, tears, breath]

Eleanor typed, waited.

Eleanor read:

I just checked on the computer and I don't seem to see any software that would allow me to burn DVD's or CD's. I am used to Toast, Daemon tools. I'm not aware of any other software that you are using! I am busy trying to download some software!

Eleanor logged out [pacing, tarot, tea]

Abraham sat at the bar [flirting, drink, book]

Time passed.

Eleanor logged in [password alert, recovery, breach]

She fumed, typed.

Abraham leaned and smoked [flirting, book]

Time passed.

She read:

Ohhhh man,

Well I don't know what he has been up too but I am sorry to hear that. I haven't seen the guy or talked to him.

I will get in contact with him but that's all I can do. I now regret having involved myself in all of this!

That's what you get for trying to help. Anyway, I can understand your motive though.

Please consider me out of this issue. Like I said that guy is not even my friend.

Have a blessed day!

PS I consider this chapter closed

Eleanor sat, stalled by this turn in the dialogue. The closing had followed so soon upon the opening, it felt almost like they'd happened in reverse.

She turned her head to the right. The dishtowel had fallen from the handle of the stove to form a maroon amoeba on the parquet floor.

She thought, Consider the towel an amoeba on the floor, and realized she'd stolen the word "consider" from Danny K.M.

Time passed. Abraham did not come home. Eleanor texted a friend about the laptop, the emails. Her friend replied: "Ug sorry, u backed up? This is why I've caved to the cloud ;/"

She texted another friend about the laptop, the emails, the password-change alerts. He responded: "The cops won't find it but if you have renters insurance you have to file a report FYI Xx."

She didn't have renters insurance, but Abraham might. She texted him, waited, texted again. She got up.

HOW OFTEN DO YOU FEEL as if you are essentially undeserving?

Do you suspect this feeling is universal?

How often do you punish yourself physically, for instance by hitting yourself, for a sin you believe you have committed but cannot identify?

How many times, per week, are you able to enjoy sex with yourself or with others?

How many times, per week, do you berate yourself, out loud or in writing, to others?

How frequently do you imagine your own funeral?

How frequently do you think others imagine their own funerals?

When you imagine your funeral, how many people are in attendance?

How do you handle the logical contradiction of believing yourself to be essentially less deserving than others while also believing you're nothing special?

How do you handle the theoretical contradiction between your atheism and your conviction that you are being punished by some unseen hand?

How often do you imagine your own death? On a scale of one to ten, how beautiful is it?

THE AIR OUTSIDE was translucent, as if particles of cold were suspended in it, and when she looked down Flatbush before turning onto Nevins she saw, sliding out from behind the Savings Bank clock tower, the moon—full or nearly full or just over being full—too big, too low, and of an ugly indeterminate color between salmon and puce. She turned. She passed by the slightly drunken couples walking arm-in-arm from dinner to the bar or from the bar to dinner. She passed by the very drunken person singing loudly as he marched up the sidewalk in a T-shirt and shorts. She paused a few blocks from the café to recall the gesture of the barista with the poorly disguised heart—around the corner and to the right—and calculated where to turn, and when she did she saw, halfway down the block, a cluster of police cars parked in front of a low brick building. She walked up to the door—to its right, faded white-painted block letters declared 9-1-1 WE WILL NOT FORGET—and pushed it open.

The desk cop looked like the hero of a romance novel from the '70s—tanned skin, thick black hair, caterpillar mustache. In the romance novel he would be a lothario, would offer schoolgirls their first lesson in lotharios. It's possible that Eleanor had read such a novel at one time, had learned something from it. The lothario cop handed her a form to fill out and she sat on a bench, pulled a pen from her bag. Then she was standing at the counter with her completed incident report in one hand and a folder containing the printouts of her email correspondence with Danny K.M. in the other. The cop put on a pair of blue plastic reading glasses and no longer looked like a lothario. He peered at Eleanor over their sparkly rims.

"You wrote a name under *Suspect* and then you crossed it out."

"I have a . . . witness, I guess, but there's no place to put down his name. I don't want him down as a suspect."

"You have a witness?"

"Someone emailed me from the stolen computer."

The cop's eyebrows rose above the rims of his glasses. The left went up higher than the right.

"The person who stole your computer emailed you, and you don't want to put him down as a suspect?"

"He's not the one who stole it. His friend probably stole it, or bought it stolen. He was trying to give me back my data. I'm just trying to file a—"

"His friend stole it?"

"I don't want to report him. It's for the insurance. I thought . . ."

Eleanor blushed at the untenability of her position. The cop leaned back in his chair and crossed his arms against his chest. Eleanor thought she could see him shake his head, just slightly, in disdain or disbelief or some prefabricated combination of the two.

"Suspect or no suspect. Those are your choices."

Eleanor, quietly: "No suspect."

"Right! Well, we'll see what we can do."

The cop, who had removed his glasses and regained some of his lotharioness, stapled together the pages of Eleanor's incident report and tossed it somewhere by his feet. Then he swiveled his chair to the right and busied himself with a stack of paperwork piled high on the long wooden desk.

If he did come home, he would be drunk. If he did not come home, she would feel indefensibly lonely—indefensibly because of their arrangement, which was as old as their relationship, and which had to do with the disavowal or at least suppression of certain feelings, specifically those of possession, jealousy, complacency.

Eleanor had left the police station and automatically turned in the direction of Abraham's apartment. The lights were on inside a newly settled stretch of boutiques, the usual influx into neighborhoods in the late stages of gentrification—designer maternity store, coffee roaster, purveyor of handmade gifts—and inside them workers swept, cashed out, turned signs from OPEN to CLOSED. The street was near empty. Her arms crossed tightly like the lothario cop's, Eleanor walked slowly, her thoughts turning from the cop to Abraham to Danny K.M.

Those are your choices.

Happens.

Please, understand.

Three teenagers overtook her from behind, shrieking and falling into each other as they raced to the block's end, trailed by the scent of pot. Possession, jealousy, complacency—these, she and her lover had agreed, were feelings that lead to unhappiness and, inevitably, despair, and they had organized their situation so as to stave them off. For Abraham, the arrangement was close to ideal.

Eleanor turned and began walking in the opposite direction.

"I know how it feels," Danny K.M. had written. Eleanor took this—a cliché, at best a well-meaning but weak speech act, like the similarly intentioned "you are not alone"—literally. She took it to mean that some person in the world, some Danny K.M., sitting in front of an ill-begotten keyboard somewhere, had felt, if only for an instant, what she felt, and had been moved to tell her so at some risk to himself, and the reciprocal fellow-feeling this gesture sparked in her was—though she was not yet able to take note of it—vast, unknowably vast and growing.

Some time ago, after the thing that happened had happened, she'd signed a month-to-month lease on a room in a house in an adjacent part of the borough. Her room was a ten-by-twelve-foot box, painted a warm brown, with a single window overlooking the polluted canal. She spent little time there now, but it was a peaceful place, with housemates who were friendly but not intrusive, and who made her feel both older (they were in their twenties) and younger than she was. Today when she entered they were sitting in the living area, their figures partially effaced by smoke, watching one of Jonas Mekas's *Walden* films on a giant laptop poised atop the coffee-table clutter.

"Hey."

"Hey."

Eleanor joined them and sank into the film, which was so beautiful—so full of tenderness and nostalgia and mute observation, of people walking on grass, sunlight caught on celluloid, kaleidoscopic portraits of beloveds—she felt herself slide away, and slide away again, and again, until it began to seem ridiculous—all of this sliding without destination—and she got up, excused herself, retired to her room, and fell asleep on the unmade bed.

In her sleep she wrote an email to Danny K.M., only fragments of which she would recall in the morning:

Dear Danny,

Have you ever
                    and then in a dream or in the shower—
        clichés
                        not even a handle
            that the problem is opening up?

                            you carry it around.
                    something will be altered

                transformed
                                the way
something sounds when you describe it
                        beyond judgment,
                            in a file called Revision

                                Something I made
happen   Do you
                    you will know everything about
me   friends
                are you there?

-eleanor

WHEN I FINALLY received word from the critic, nearly a week had passed since he'd left for his tour. I was juggling stress at work (my supervising editor at the magazine had been indicted for fraud) and at home: my girlfriend, Kat, and I were separating, and she'd moved into what had been our shared office until she could find a new place to live.

I spent whatever free time I had revising the first section of my manuscript, though I found myself also reading up on the dangers—mainly immune-related, as the critic had suggested—of "sub-optimal genetic diversity." Our night at the bar had both intensified and complicated my interest in the critic: he was self-absorbed and entitled (Kat would sneer *narc!* and run), but there were introspection, curiosity, and vulnerability there too, and the combination, when mixed with our secret history, touched me. That I couldn't tell to what degree he was flirting with me specifically or with me as a genre didn't matter, since my interest in that part of our dynamic was (and not only because he was engaged and I was mostly off men) academic, and I was determined to keep it so.

He had sent me, before leaving, his itinerary, so I could share his amusement at the language it contained. It had been written in imperfect English by the PR person for his Swedish distributor who was (inexplicably, he said, as Sweden is full of fluent English speakers) a native Austrian, recently migrated to the north. The list of screenings and interviews and luncheons was punctuated by the kind of inadvertent innuendo—"We hope you will be satisfied by your escort," "The menus have been designed to your affections"—that only the resolutely monolingual would ridicule, and I remembered that this Beckett expert had failed (though he claimed to have tried) to learn French. In the flurry of messages we exchanged after our night at the bar, he hadn't mentioned the dilemma he'd divulged there, nor did I bring it up—I didn't know how. So I was both surprised and not surprised by what he wrote to me now.

I am still in Stockholm but tomorrow I'll be in Copenhagen, wishing I were in Christiania. I have always wanted to see Christiania, and I asked my distributors if they could arrange it, but they said no. Do you know what happens in Christiania. It has become Disneyland. But you can still buy hash.

I am drunk. They have given me a lot of aquavit. They have given it to me at dinner, and they have left it in my room. I have drunk the aquavit they left in my room. I have drunk it all. It was a small bottle. It tasted like a tonic. I drank it to cure my ills.

I have been spending time with my handler. She told me she hates experimental documentary. She's a self-described left-populist who believes in TV. I don't think she hated my film but I think she wanted to. Hate it. She reminds me of you. Do you hate my film.

That was the end of the first email, but a second followed immediately.

I'm not really drunk. I haven't told Laurance anything. When I left for the airport she said, *I love you, you know.* My handler is pregnant, I mean she is very very pregnant. Big as a house. Laurance doesn't want kids, but I've always thought I'd have three. Tell me what I'm supposed to do.

The brochure says *Dogs run wild and play in the narrow streets where no cars are allowed. The mild scent of cannabis is in the air when you walk through the famous Pusher Street. Groups of foreign tourists on guided tours blend in with chilled-out youngsters and the locals who work in the various small shops and cafees where you can pay with a special Christiania currency.*

I would like the opportunity to buy hash as part of a guided tour.

I want to go to a *cafee.*

I am lost.

There was a third email in the same thread but sent, according to the time stamp, two hours later. I could see that it was long, and I went and poured myself a glass of wine—a third glass of wine; it was after dinner and I was alone—before beginning to read.

You realize that you are now—for how long I don't know, but at least for now, and possibly for all time—in a category, with relation to my biography, all by yourself. I have been thinking about this. Because, what do you really know about me: That I wrestled in school, that I like to drink whiskey. That I'm shit at maths. What do I know about you: even less. What I know about you—what I know about you could fit on a Post-it note. Could fit on a postage stamp. Could fit on the head of a pin. I barely know how to pronounce your name. Is your name Russian. How do you pronounce your name.

When I was twelve—this was in a suburb of Madison, Wisconsin, during the years my dad was a postdoc—there was a kid in my class named Sasha. He was one of three boys from Moscow who had come over at the same time. The others were Yuri and Boris, I kid you not. It was around the time that Sting song came out, you remember—"I hope the Russians love their children too"—and the whole experience, these three Russkies coming to this midwestern school—we called it the Russian invasion—was a formative event for a lot of the kids in my class. I don't think anyone else even understood that they were Jews—that that's why they had left the Soviet Union, they were the children of dissidents, they'd been pushed out—but my family was European and political so somehow we knew. I became friends with them, with Sasha especially—he was a wrestler too, we were both in the same weight class, 103 lbs if you can believe that—and we would sit together in the cafeteria. We smoked grass for the first time together too, a roach I'd nicked from my sister (do you even know I have a sister) in the alley behind the school with a homeless guy taking a shit ten feet away. The Russkies and I and a couple of girls from our class (that's a different story: the girls, Lizette Tanikawa . . .) all volunteered for the Walter Mondale campaign in the fall of '84. I think the Russian parents leaned Republican, the Cold War Reaganite thing, but since the sons were friends with me, and though my parents couldn't vote they liked to lecture kids about the fragility of democracy—do you remember how the yuppies all fell hard for trickle-down?—the young

Russians joined up. We rode around after school in a van and offered people lawn signs, that kind of thing. I can't remember who was driving the van, I guess some older volunteer. One day, after we'd run out of signs, we asked to be dropped off at the lake, and we were all messing around; the girls were flirting with Sasha and Yuri, who were the attractive ones, and Boris—who had a sort of capsized face—and I were throwing rocks at the little waves, trying to land them right on the break. The sun was going down and creating this glare from the water, so I couldn't see that Sasha and one of the girls— Colleen, or Corrine, I've managed to forget—were crouched together at the shore's edge, and I hurled a rock in the air and it was the best throw I had probably ever executed in my life, and Boris and I looked up as it arced across the variegated pink and orange sky, and then Sasha was flat on the sand and blood was everywhere.

He survived, but with impaired speech and cognition. It turned out he was epileptic—the family had been hiding it. They didn't press charges, but his parents wouldn't let me near him anymore. When we finally saw each other on his front lawn on Yom Kippur, he attempted a single leg takedown, which I countered with a poorly executed sprawl. We both laughed a little, and then he went back inside. My family returned to London that spring. Sasha died after a grand mal seizure the week the rest of them graduated high school.

The sun is coming up. My window looks out over the Stockholm archipelago. Boat masts swaying. Kayaks being let into the sea. A kid throwing rocks, or is he dancing. The colors—what I notice—what any of us notices—

The string of emails ended there. I finished my glass of wine, wandered out of habit into what had been the office, stumbling immediately into a pile of Kat's vintage stilettos, and looked out the window at the illuminated street. I took a picture of what I saw and emailed it to the critic with the caption "for the Post-it, more soon."

AMONG THE THINGS Abraham knows about Eleanor: She's a boring dresser. She's aroused by sleeping in public. She reads fitfully but often. She cries on the subway. She's hopeless at math. She's fond of sex toys, especially vibrators, blindfolds, nipple clamps, and anything made of fur. Her favorite thing to watch on television is reruns of *M*A*S*H*.

Among the things Eleanor knows about Abraham: He hates the word "practice" as a stand-in for "work." He knows his way around the butchering of a chicken. He has an extra vertebra in his lower back. He can take or leave most sex toys—cock rings, blindfolds, clamps—though he enjoys the use of restraints. He watches television in hotels, where he favors sports, news, and porn.

Among the things Eleanor knows about Danny K.M.:
"Please, understand that I am trying to help."
"I consider this chapter closed."

Among the things Danny K.M. knows about Eleanor:

DEVICES
  iDisk
  Google SketchUp 6.0 Installer
SHARED
  PLACES
    Dropbox
  Desktop
  Noteleanor
  Documents
  Applications
SEARCH FOR
  Today
  Yesterday
  Past Week
  All Images
  All Movies
  All Documents

SPRING BREAK FELL unusually close to the end of the semester, and under ordinary circumstances Eleanor would have spent it at cafés with her laptop fielding emails from a few overly ambitious students already worrying about their final grades. Now—the week lost to the occurrence and effects of thing #2, and consequently to the renewed repercussions of the first thing, thing-prime—except when she was at Abraham's apartment, she had to field emails on her phone. On the Saturday before break ended, she thumb-typed a message to Danny K.M. She was barefoot and freshly showered, sprawled on the bed in her brown room; the window was cracked open to welcome a tentative spring breeze from the canal.

> Dear Danny,
> I understand that you don't want to be in touch. I understand that you feel you've done all you can do. I appreciate that you wanted to help me, I do. I believe your intentions are good. Most of what I lost on that laptop I can live without, but there is one document I would like very much to see again [. . .]

She finished her email and hit "Send," and then she checked the news. She was still following the story of the Tampa Bay movie house shooting—following it above other stories she believed were more important, stories of revolution and corruption and race and class war. She followed it for reasons she could scarcely defend to herself. Maybe it was a question of scale; the story felt small enough to psychically manage. The facts of the case were few: The motive was annoyance at public texting. The shooter was charged with second-degree murder. The lethal bullet had also grazed the hand of the victim's wife, which she had raised in an effort to protect her husband. The wife's name was Nicole. She was in her early forties. He was a good, genuine person. Their daughter was three.

She read some poems that were posted to a blog she sometimes looked at. The poems were about revolution, corruption, race, and class war. She agreed with the poems—nodding along as she read—but she felt, simultaneous with the nodding and just as involuntarily, a familiar sense that agreement wasn't enough.

She looked up second-degree murder:

1) an intentional killing that is not premeditated or planned, nor committed in a reasonable "heat of passion," or 2) a killing caused by dangerous conduct and the offender's obvious lack of concern for human life.

As Eleanor wondered what might count as a "reasonable heat of passion," Abraham texted to ask if she was coming to see him that night. Her last free days passed much like this, and then they were over.

Her students, apart from the overly ambitious ones, returned refreshed from vacation or were still away, so she had small, focused classes and enjoyed her first days back, until inertia took over and she began to count the weeks to semester's end.

She had received no response from Danny K.M., no phone call from the police. The value of her lost data, though it contained years' worth of unarchived photographs and more, had been reduced in her mind to the twenty pages of notes in the document she'd asked Danny to send, the contents of which she could scarcely recall. Paragraphs, disjointed and belonging to no fixed genre, that she had written over the course of the past year, that she had saved on the desktop rather than in one of the directories she backed up at random intervals to an old hard drive, because there was no place in her directories where the paragraphs belonged—not "Freelance," not "Teaching," not "Dissertation_notes" (the latter had been moribund for years, since she abandoned her thesis and her program after, like a sick child, *failing to thrive*). Despite what she had imagined writing to Danny K.M. in her dream, despite what she had actually written to Danny K.M., she did not engage in magical thinking about these paragraphs. She did not believe that they could transform her, even that they could help her to "process" the thing that had happened. What she believed, what she knew, was that with them she had built a site for a certain kind of thinking that was difficult but necessary for her to do, and that deprived of the site she had built for it, that kind of thinking was now—perhaps dangerously—at large.

The final project she had assigned her Modern World Lit students was a comparative essay about *Woman at Point Zero* by Nawal El Saadawi and *Forever Valley* by Marie Redonnet. The novels were short and among her favorites, so she had put them on the syllabus without as much consideration as, she now realized, was merited. Overall, the drafts she received reflected either a basic understanding of the conventional essay form but a lack of insight into the novels themselves, or the converse. "Woman throughout time have been pushed down by a male dominated society as depicted by the cultural backgrounds of the two novels, one in the Arab world and one of fiction," began one. Another contained this sentence, which Eleanor puzzled over at lunch one afternoon, sitting on a bench in the hall outside the office she shared with too many other adjuncts to make it useful to any of them: "The narrator of *Forever Vally* is poor and illiterate but not stupid, in fact not reading can mean being smart, which is the case with this character who sold her soul using sex so she can do her project; to dig a hole that has no meaning but is meaningful anyways to her, alas."

It was the final "alas" that Eleanor could not understand, and she tried to reproduce an image of the student whose name was at the top of the paper but no face came to mind, and only when she checked her attendance roster did she confirm that this student, who had written a paper twice as long as the five-page minimum, a paper full of ideas—chaotically expressed but ingeniously developed—had attended her fifteen-week class exactly once.

She recalled a past class, years earlier, in which she had also assigned *Woman at Point Zero*, and one of her students had written a critical analysis of empathy in the relationship between the narrator and the imprisoned protagonist, Firdaus, that made her weep.

Maybe fiction is a cultural background, she thought as she finished her peanut butter sandwich. What do I know?

Maybe I should dig a hole, she thought as she got up, crumpled the napkin she'd wrapped her sandwich in and, not finding a garbage can nearby, tucked it in her bag. Alas.

ELEANOR KNEW OF the artist and of some of her previous performances: the one in which she carved a pentagram into her abdomen which she whipped until it bled, and the one in which she and her lover walked from opposite ends of the Great Wall of China toward each other, for three months, only to meet in the middle and break up. Eleanor, conscious that she was in danger of losing herself completely to the intensified repercussions of thing-prime as brought on by the vicissitudes of thing #2, had decided to take a break from all of it to see the artist's new show, the one everyone was talking about, that was being advertised on the sides of buses and on posters in subway cars. She took one of those subway cars, was nearly felled by tourists stopping short on the escalator, and stepped into the bright and crowded streets. There was a line for the exhibit and Eleanor joined it, taking her place behind a group of three young bored-looking women in pastel clogs and an elderly man with watery azure eyes.

She had friends who hated the artist and friends who were obsessed with her; one friend, who shared with the artist both her national provenance and a childhood similarly devoid of love, was transformed so much by the experience of looking into her eyes that for the last two months she'd been wandering from state to state, deepening her already substantial credit card debt to stage performances that tried her physical and emotional limits. In one, she erected a twig teepee near the eighteenth hole of a five-star golf course in Montana—her absentee father had been a semi-pro golfer—and spent a freezing night there, braving skunks and the shadow of the Unabomber, only to wake to a confrontation with security guards that resulted in her returning home with swaths of black and blue on her wrists and a contusion on her right leg.

Eleanor squinted at her phone, on which she'd called up the museum's website, and read ["re-performance," "retrospective," "audience participation," "1946," "opening hours"].

She searched the title of the exhibition and found a series of blogs devoted to it. She read ["life-changing," "pretentious," "cried and cried"].

Time passed. Eleanor crept toward the head of the line.

Time passed. The group that contained Eleanor was let into the museum and flowed as one past the exhibits and to the gallery where the artist was present, and where the artwork—herself, seated at a table—was on display. The line of people waiting to sit across from the artist was long, but it was different from the line outside, in that most of the people in it were sitting rather than standing, and whereas outside the people had no single thing to look at, their attention divided between the streets of the city and each other, inside they had a singular thing to watch: the artist and her performance.

Eleanor watched a man approach the artist and sit. The artist lifted her eyes and held the man's gaze. The man had a thick black mustache, not unlike the lothario cop's, though he was skinnier and he looked, Eleanor caught herself thinking, more soulful. He sat for five minutes, wept, and left.

She watched a young woman approach the artist. The young woman, who was wearing a summery dress, who could have been one of Eleanor's students but wasn't, did not sit down right away as had the mustachioed man but remained standing in front of the artist, then reached down and grabbed the hemline of her dress, pulling it over her head to reveal her naked body, a pale and thin, young body, which was seized immediately by two large security guards who appeared from nowhere, whisking it—the body—away from the artist, who had lowered her head already and closed her eyes, the gesture she'd come to make, not impolitely, when gathering herself between encounters.

Elsewhere in the exhibit, a naked woman hung from a peg on the wall as if from a bicycle seat. Elsewhere in the exhibit, a naked woman lay beneath a human skeleton, in the missionary position. Elsewhere in the exhibit a man and a woman, and then a man and a man, and then a woman and a woman stood facing each other on opposite sides of a narrow doorway, naked, forcing museum visitors, even the slimmest among them, to choose one of the bodies to touch with their front side, and another with their backside, as they squeezed through the narrow opening.

Eleanor did not want to take off her dress, though it was warm in the room, which looked more like a film set—or what Eleanor imagined a film set to look like—than like an exhibition space or even a performance space, and she concluded that the lights that were making the space look like a film set were also the cause of the warmth, though not the cause of the young woman's desire to make herself naked in front of the artist. The young woman was now standing not far from where Eleanor sat and was being interviewed by a man with a large video camera, a professional with a fuzzy microphone and an assistant, and she, the woman, was weeping and gesticulating and explaining that she didn't mean any disrespect but wanted only to make herself as vulnerable in front of the artist as the artist was claiming to be in front of her. She only wanted to take the artist at her word.

Eleanor took out her pen and wrote on her palm: *relational aesthetics book.*

She put away her pen. She watched.

She took out her pen and wrote on her wrist: *milk granola tampons.*

She did not get the opportunity to sit in front of the artist and gaze into her eyes. She wasn't far from the front of the line, but the person three spots ahead of her had taken seventy-six minutes, and the person two spots ahead of her had taken forty-three minutes, and the person just ahead of her had sat down for ten minutes and then was escorted out, along with Eleanor and everybody else except the artist herself, by a guard who intoned somberly that the museum was closing and they were welcome to come back tomorrow.

Eleanor would not come back tomorrow. She did not know what she thought of the artist and her project. She disliked the vitriol some directed at her, but she couldn't seem to come wholly to the artist's defense, even in the privacy of her mind. She thought of the well-known artists about whom she had changed or solidified her opinion after meeting one of their assistants and finding out how often they yelled and how much they paid.

She looked again at the middle-aged woman who had been sitting for seven hours locking eyes with strangers, a few friends and acquaintances surely among them. The artist seemed sad, and Eleanor wondered what the thing was that had happened to her, that she had caused or not-caused or that was beyond her control, and as she kept looking at the artist over her shoulder, even as she was being ushered out of the gallery with the other museumgoers who either had or had not been given the chance to lock eyes with the artist, Eleanor felt her life lift a few millimeters away from her skin, as if attracted by a magnetic field suddenly encircling only her and the artist; and the vibrating feeling of her life as it hovered near her skin gave her a sensation of nearness to the artist about whose work she was ambivalent, so that with each step of increasing distance she felt closer to the artist and farther from her ambivalence, as if the artist was both the source of and solution to that ambivalence—until the door to the exhibition hall closed behind her, and without any transition the field was dissolved and her life fell back into her skin and her ambivalence returned and she no longer felt close to the artist but very far away.

DAYLIGHT SAVINGS BEGAN; night fell later. People who had spent months beneath wool hats and scarves got haircuts, went shopping for clothes in bright colors and pale neutrals—especially pale neutrals since the shows that year were full of beige, ecru, and taupe, a fact she knew only because a talkative friend's livelihood depended on it. Eleanor too went shopping one day and bought a silk-blend dress—in taupe—which she would not be able to wear until the weather warmed another fifteen degrees, but which she kept on a hanger slung over a nail in the door to her room, the tag from the sample sale still attached.

She went back to her books. She read *Two Serious Ladies* and *The Descent of Alette*. She read parts of *Reader's Block* and of *Wittgenstein's Mistress*. She read almost all of *Wittgenstein's Nephew* and started *Rameau's Nephew* again. She thought about projects and their abandonment. Her missing paragraphs nagged. Time passed.

She had received no reply from Danny K.M. The closer she got to "letting go" of thing #2, the more forcefully the thing that had happened before returned. When she tried on the dress in a shared dressing room beside strangers, it was there. When she walked in slow motion from her room to the bathroom, where the shower provided barely a trickle of warm water in the afternoons, it was there. When she rode the subway and regarded the faces across from her, she thought she saw evidence in each of them of a thing that had happened, that they had caused or not-caused and that could come back to crush them; she got caught staring, trying to imagine what the thing, in each case, might be.

Often she saw, superimposed on one of the strangers' faces, an image from a Cassavetes film—she couldn't remember which one—in which a woman stares at her reflection, drunk, her made-up face maligned by tears, wailing from some unidentified pain unknowable even to her. (What she didn't realize, but you may, is that she was confusing scenes and cineastes, that she had conflated the shot of the streaked makeup on the wailing woman from the party scene in *Breakfast at Tiffany's* with one of any number of scenes in Cassavetes's films—for instance, the dressing-room scene from *Opening Night* in which Gena Rowlands's aging actress, Myrtle, witnesses her fragmentation in an array of mirrors.)

And what can be said about Abraham? Eleanor had very little to say about Abraham. During this time, when she was back at work and preoccupied (in a last-ditch effort to increase her effectiveness) with helping her students revise their papers and prepare their final portfolios, she saw her lover only every third or fourth night.

She was aware of what might look like a lack of intimacy in their proceedings. When they fucked they didn't look at each other, they didn't talk: there was what you might call an instrumentality to the thing. But she rejected the theory—put forth by one of her male friends with whom she occasionally discussed her relationship—that her reliance on toys and props and nonmutual fantasy play was itself indicative of a suboptimal level of intimacy. She and her lover were not perfectly matched, she was the first to admit. He couldn't read her mind, and she didn't want to instruct; often he did the right thing at the wrong time. But neither did she recognize a simple opposition between (to use the words of her theorizing friend) technology and authenticity. Even when pressed, she couldn't come up with meaningful definitions for either term, the first becoming so broad it seemed to encompass almost everything, and the second so narrow it disappeared under the vaguest pressure. Whereas when Eleanor imagined superimposing the image of the distraught woman—not exactly an image, but a complex pastiche—onto the faces of strangers, she felt certain that she was extending something real to them, which meant only something living, as authentic or inauthentic as flesh-to-flesh contact, as placing her hands on theirs.

She read *The Left-Handed Woman*. She read *Don't Let Me Be Lonely* and *Ana Patova Crosses a Bridge,* which she immediately read again. She read *Creature* and *The Pirate Who Does Not Know the Value of Pi.* She read the first three chapters of *Dawn*. She fell asleep, content, her cheek resting on the page.

What is the essence of really good sex? she read on her phone at the café when she should have been grading.

- Really good sex has no guilt or shame coming with it.
- Really good sex is not just about relief of tension or anxiety, but entails positive emotions such as love and emotional intimacy.
- Really good sex arouses feelings that last much longer than the span of the moment. The afterglow can last for hours or days.
- Really good sex is experienced at a much deeper level than sex that is casual. It has meaning because it is connected to important values.

- Really good sex is mutually enjoyable, it is not a one-way street. Each partner takes a selfish pleasure in both getting and receiving.

She wondered if "getting" was a typo for "giving" or a Freudian slip, and then she wondered if the authors or algorithms responsible for articles like these were vulnerable to Freudian slips, and then she put down her phone.

Time passed. Eleanor taught, walked, visited the library. She found a first edition of *Maud Martha* on the reference shelf and read it in an afternoon. One morning, she received a surprise package: a box of unsold sale items from an ex-roommate who'd moved to San Francisco to work at Good Vibrations.

Time passed.

Abraham [goggles, measuring tape, SKILSAW]

They had sex using the Intima Silk Blindfold and the black ostrich feather.

Time passed. Eleanor taught, walked, sat in the park with a friend.

Abraham [hammer drill, router, glue]

They had sex using the Sidekick Silicone Anal Plug and the Nipple Teasers Vibrating Nipple Clamps. Eleanor's thoughts when she came flashed to Danny K.M.

Time passed. Eleanor taught, walked, read the news on the internet. She read about protesters in Syria and upheaval in Athens.

Abraham [cigarette, flirting, goggles]

They had sex using the Bound to Please Neoprene Restraints and the Naughty and Nice Plush Paddle. With Velcro straps holding her ankles and wrists to the bed, Eleanor took the pleasure of both getting and receiving; the afterglow lasted for hours, lasted for days.

"Me and my husband didn't get a date night very often," said the wife of the victim of the Tampa Bay shooting to reporters. "It's just so hard and so unbearable."

When all the toys had been used in most of their permutations, Eleanor and Abraham sat down.

Abraham said something to the effect of I need some space.

Eleanor responded.

Abraham said something to the effect of I have a lot to do to get ready for my trip—he had been planning a month-long motorcycle trip along the Trans-Labrador Highway in Canada, an adventure that apparently required a great deal of preparation, mostly by sitting in front of a computer ordering specialty gear—and I don't want to feel the pressure of being a good boyfriend.

These were not the actual words he used, you understand.

Eleanor stared.

Abraham reassured her to the tune of I don't want us to stop seeing each other completely.

The next day, she collected her students' portfolios. One student, a woman Eleanor's age who had three children and was trying to complete an abandoned BA, had brought her a homemade brownie. She ate the brownie while walking down the fluorescent corridor to the faculty mailboxes to pick up her final paycheck for the semester. Then she walked two blocks with her head down, counting the number of broken bottles in the gutter—eleven—to the student union store where she bought, on credit, from an aloof former student, a refurbished laptop with a carrying case. Then she walked three miles through the dissolving light to the adjacent part of the borough, where she unpacked her new computer in her brown box of a room.

I WAS BEGINNING to wonder what was really going on with the critic. He was writing often now, at least four or five times each day, and the messages were becoming less and less legible: noisier, as if complicated by static. I responded to his story about Sasha with an equally revealing if less dramatic childhood tale of my own—hoping this would restore an equilibrium to our friendship—and he continued to ask for and comment on pages of my novel as I made progress on its revision. I had become convinced he would never remember me from that long-ago class unless I prompted him (and I seemed to enjoy not doing so); I'd become convinced, too, that his interest in reading my text so closely was, though not completely scrutable, genuine. But I noticed that his increased attentiveness—which I admit kept me company as I got used to watching Kat come and go, mostly go, with her suddenly numerous young friends—was accompanied by an increased evasiveness. I asked him directly more than once to update me about Laurance and whether he'd opted to take the gene test: no reply. I sent a one-line email: "Have you talked to your mother?" and he responded by texting me a picture of himself on Pusher Street in Christiania, where he had finally convinced his Danish distributors to take him on his afternoon off.

It was after midnight on a Sunday when I received his selfie, and I'd been working on my revision since morning. My writing had been interrupted several times already by the emails he'd sent every few hours during the day, presumably from his phone. I was incapable of ignoring the incoming messages; even when I went offline for stretches, whenever I did check my in-box, the most recent message would be from him. He seemed to write spontaneously and not to reread before sending, and what I could discern through the typos and autocorrects and missing words was that he had gotten his hands on a lot of hash, which he was smoking regularly in semihiding while being ferried from one press event to another by an assortment of interns, invariably young and handsome. He would write to me after being interviewed by journalists and talk-show hosts he described interchangeably as "perfectly nice," "morons," or "loons," often providing something of the nature of the interaction—the questions were straight from the press release, the host had not seen the film, the interviewer looked like she was fourteen—but mostly he would share a detail of whatever environment he was in when he wrote, informing me in his offhandedly pedantic way of the amenities in the men's bathroom, the specifics of Scandinavian hotel porn, the average height of the people drinking at the bar. He switched rapidly between topics within a single message: He'd seen an intriguing exhibit in Malmö by the artist-in-residence on a research vessel owned by a French fashion designer that had been ice-locked near the North Pole for the better part of a year; his description of her photograph of ice fissures lit from below led to a quote from the poet Inger Christensen that he'd encountered in a bookstore window—"I always thought reality / was something you became / when you grew up"—which led in turn to a critique of the social media activities of someone we both vaguely knew, which reminded him of everything wrong with the world today.

In the photo, only about two-thirds of his face was visible in the frame; he was evidently holding his phone at arm's length to provide a view of the market behind him, identifiable not only by the signage and general vibe of the crowd but by some extravisual quality that came across through the screen, improbably, as smell.

I typed something to the effect of You look happy there; I wish I could see all the places you're seeing, to which he replied something to the effect of The thing about the smorgasbord is there's only the illusion of choice. I typed something to the effect of Sometimes your comments on my pages are overbearing, though I'm grateful for them, to which he replied with a picture of a dog with three legs and pink-dyed fur. Our conversation continued in this way until a feeling I'd been slowly identifying over the previous weeks began to solidify into an image of myself as a prop, an actual prop—a bottle of fake whiskey, or a plastic gun—in the critic's drama of transformation, a drama which (though I didn't doubt its authenticity) was beginning to read as farce. My role as prop, moreover, was usurping my role as significant new friend—itself a part I'd been cast in, not exactly against my will but also not as a result of it, on the day he chose to let me in on his family secret—and when I formulated this thought to myself I typed something to the effect of I feel sick, to which he replied It's starting to rain. Finally, I realized the only way I could cleave some air between my thoughts and the anxious influence of the critic would be by deliberately, and not without difficulty, falling silent for a while.

IN ONE AFTERNOON Eleanor picked up and discarded *The Uprising,*
Gunslinger II, The Wisdom of Sustainability, and *Why the Child Is*
Cooking in the Polenta. She was propped up on her bed, the door to
her room closed against the clutter of her absent housemates, the
window swung open to a cloudless day. It was the first of June. She
had at last put on the taupe dress, though she had no plans to go
out, and was wearing it still, its white cardboard tag dangling from
a sleeve. A pile of books took up half of her double bed, the space
of a human being.

This was how she'd spent the days since she collected her final paycheck and cashed it, and since Abraham asked, not in these words
but effectively, for some space. She read the news on the internet,
maxing out her free page views on the corporate sites, maxing out
her tolerance of user-generated content on the far-left and far-right
blogs she felt compelled to read in tandem, as if doing so would
somehow grant her a more complete picture of the world as it really
was. She read opinions on both sides of the gun debate, the immi-
gration debate, the copyright debate, the Indian casino debate, the
domestic drone debate. She was unable to muster any of the outrage
she expected to feel at the opinions she read, leaning instead toward
the seductive embrace of sleep.

She had lately found herself envisioning a life in which the thing
that had happened had not happened at all, a parallel life unfolding

next to the one she was living, next to it but not visible from it, a coyote in the shadows beside the road. She would awaken from a nap and feel uncertain which life she was in, the one she knew or the one she envisioned, and the two would toggle back and forth for a time, like when she used to wake up in bed next to one body and for a few seconds believe it belonged to someone else.

She wept often and openly at her imaginings, while knowing that any coherent theory of parallel lives would not support such acute grieving, that the Twin Earth thought experiment as proposed by Hilary Putnam in a book she'd pulled recently from her pile called *The Meaning of "Meaning"* was instead concerned with the question of reference, of whether a twin-Eleanor to whom something different but identically affecting had happened—something that left an imprint on her mental and emotional state that was identical to the imprint left by the thing that had happened on Eleanor herself, identical even on the molecular level—whether that twin-Eleanor, when she referred to the thing that had happened, could be said to be referring to the selfsame thing to which Eleanor, so often, if only to herself, and especially during the days she was now spending alone in her room, referred.

The answer, for Putnam, was no. Eleanor and twin-Eleanor, though they might be having virtually, even molecularly indistinguishable experiences, could not be said to be having those experiences *about* the same thing.

Added to this was the problem that whenever Eleanor read the word "causality" she mistook it for "casualty" and found her mind populated with images of untreated wounds and detached limbs, images that were common on the front pages of the news sites that purported to tell the true and complete story of the world as it really was. The result was that whatever acute grief Eleanor felt or almost felt when her thoughts turned to the thing that had happened— whatever sense of alienated proximity or proximate alienation she had cultivated, albeit unconsciously, in relation to the thing—was never quite fully expressed, even to herself, despite the open and frequent weeping, despite the diagnosably extreme seductions of sleep. It was never fully expressed because never singularly caused: any rational person when confronted with the spate of school shootings, murderous cops and their defenders, and remote-controlled bombings of unarmed civilians—and those were only the major headlines, and only this week—would be excused for believing that the particular referent, any day's unique tragedy, was of little importance, if any at all.

Between picking up and discarding books and reading the news on the internet, she would take out her Pocket Rocket. Across the canal was a red brick warehouse that had been renovated into upmarket lofts, and as she availed herself of the compact instrument's efficiency, she would leave her window open and her curtains tied back, though it was unclear to her what, if anything, could be seen from the lofts' windows without the aid of some sort of technology.

On this afternoon as she sat on the bed, half-reclined and wearing her taupe silk-blend dress, wearing also a pair of transparent stockings held up by clips and a belt because of a scene she remembered or thought she did, she chose one of the loft windows—the fourth floor in the center—and positioned herself with respect to it and to her own window to occupy center frame. She also had three windows open on her new laptop: Iraq Veterans Against the War, the e-book of *My Struggle: Vol. I,* which everyone suddenly was reading, and the search results page for "lone survivor" + "war" + "porn." She wasn't reading in any of those windows now; she wasn't reading the books piled on her bed; she was working the Rocket slowly down the front of her dress and across the tops of her stockings; she was not swinging her actual leg, but she was swinging a projection of her leg in her mind, just as she was not reading the reviews of *Lone Survivor* but was reviewing them in her mind; she could not actually see the inhabitant of the loft across the way—the art director or real-estate broker or whoever could afford to rent it— but she saw him nonetheless—business-suited, *a married man or a widower who had lost his wife or some tragedy,* nose to glass, hands in pockets as he put away his phone—as a projection in her mind; and she did not catch her knee in her hand, but she saw herself catch it; and the instrument she employed expertly came around the bottom edge of her dress, and as she worked with it she thought about the subset of returning vets whose PTSD has led to impotence; she thought—against her will—about the lothario cop, his sparkly glasses and folded arms and his incomprehension; she thought about Danny K.M. and her unanswered letter to him and about his likely compromised legal status in her country of citizenship; she thought about how she might be able to help him find a job, then was ashamed at her thought and then angered by her shame; she thought about the scene she'd just read in *My Struggle* in which an adolescent Karl Ove discovers his sexual maturity in his pants; and she thought about Pina Bausch's dancers embracing and falling, fighting the dead weight of their supplicant limbs; and as she was thinking these things, and as she was wielding the instrument in the manner for which it was designed, the figure in the loft—she actually saw this, you understand—threw open the warehouse window across the canal, and at that instant the sun dropped into the view from her room, causing a glare to reflect off the water, and something, a rock or tennis shoe or bottle, was hurled out the loft window in her general direction, and she looked up at the thing, which meant looking up at the sun, and before

she could instinctively turn away she saw the object's indeterminate silhouette arc through the air, travel up and then down toward
the polluted water, where, dropping below the bottom edge of her
frame, it vanished.

She got up and walked to the window, adjusting the waistband
of her dress. A kayak floated silently down the canal. The woman
in the kayak saw her watching and waved. Eleanor lifted her hand.

2
SUMMER

SOME PEOPLE HAVE the experience of feeling that other people, objects, and the world around them are not real. Some people have the experience of feeling that their body does not seem to belong to them. Some people have the experience of sometimes remembering a past event so vividly that they feel as if they were reliving that event. Some people find that they sometimes sit staring off into space, thinking of nothing, and are not aware of the passage of time. Some people sometimes feel as if they are looking at the world through a fog so that people and objects appear faraway or unclear.

She let her hand fall after waving to the kayaker, who had turned and was drifting down the canal, dispersing multicolored flotsam through the surface scum, as a barge breaks through ice.

The image of ice reminded Eleanor of Abraham, who had left that morning for his motorcycle trip north. They'd said goodbye the night before over a hash cigarette and the TARA Rotating Rechargeable Couples' Vibrator, and she'd returned to her room to sleep so he could spend the night packing and repacking supplies.

Time passed. She walked and read and visited friends. Those whose work didn't die off in summer invited her to concerts and lunch and drinks, but her paycheck had gone to rent, student loans, and the phone, and she stopped accepting invitations when she grew tired of not being able to pay. She entered a phase of exclusively remote conversation with a small subset of her friends, consisting mostly of text messages to the effect of "miss u" and "lets see eo soon, been 2 long!" These interactions seemed to satisfy the needs of all parties, as if the standard by which friendship required embodied interaction really was passé, as if it wasn't just her friendships that were changing but the nature of friendship itself that had changed. She scanned the results of an Amazon search for books on the subject: scant offerings providing little solace with titles like *The Friendship Book, The Friendship Crisis, How to Win Friends and Influence People in the Digital Age,* &tc.

Abraham's departure and her own retreat from sociality simplified Eleanor's daily life, exposing previously occupied territory that was reconquered almost immediately by the thing that had happened. In these moments its effects were undiminished; it seemed to have no half-life, was less like radium than like inflation, compounding interest, or a malignant tumor, subject not to exponential delay but to what she'd once learned in anthropology class to call "doubling time."

She never knew when it would come back to slay her. It could inflect equally any scene or encounter, regardless of content-relevance. On a corner near her apartment, outside the mediocre bagel shop to which she remained unaccountably loyal, for example, she ran into an acquaintance with a new baby, and the acquaintance handed her the baby, which was less than a month old, which nestled into Eleanor's shoulder and fell promptly asleep, its hand digging into her neck; and the acquaintance said to her, Eleanor, you should be a mother.

But Eleanor didn't want to be a mother. She knew too many of them, and they were too much the same. The ones who weren't the same before they were mothers became the same after. It wasn't that they talked too much about their children; what bothered her about the mothers was something more diffuse, something—she was not conscious of this structure of feeling even as it overcame her—that reproduced an aspect of the effect of the thing that had happened. It was like the feeling she got surfing the internet the way she used to, or waking from a dream set in an alternate universe of the past. But the feeling she got when she spent too much time with the mothers, individually or severally, did not originate in her as a habit or a projection; it was a by-product of the feeling the mothers themselves gave off, most strongly but not exclusively when they compared the *before* to the *after* of the era of unconditional love they felt for their spawn.

It was something about the certainty with which they asserted this shift. Her reaction was to the certainty itself.

She checked email into the night, monitoring her bodily response to each click. Mostly she felt numb, except when she would reread the thread of her correspondence with Danny K.M., which spurred a flickering near her diaphragm, a jolt. She would eventually tire, then wake at dawn in her chair, her cheek on the CAPS LOCK key.

No more security breaches had occurred. Nothing, apparently, had been done with her data. Nor had the single file she'd requested been sent, and though she considered trying to re-create the paragraphs therein—to rebuild a site for the thinking that had now been free-floating, dangerously, for weeks—she could not. Her paralysis around the paragraphs was physical too: when she thought about them, her arteries turned to ice. She formed ideas about Danny; the ideas spread like a thaw.

One night in the middle of June, she woke to the sound of her housemate grinding metal in the living room. The sound prompted a shift in Eleanor that she experienced as a minor organ some- where in her lower torso moving approximately one half inch to the left. She put in earplugs, took down the taupe dress, and detached the safety-pinned tag. She opened the top drawer of her dresser and removed a small envelope containing a new credit card she'd vowed not to use, picked up her phone, and called the number on the sticker to activate the account. She typed two words into her laptop, waited.

This was not the first time she'd searched Danny K.M.'s name; it was the first thing she'd done after receiving his initial email. She'd found only one trace of him then, enough to verify a scant if convincing online presence, but little more: a question about unlocking iPhones posted to a hacking listserv. From this she did not conclude that he was a petty technocriminal, manifestly capable of stealing her laptop, but, rather, that he had told the truth about one thing at least—his familiarity with Apple products—and this act of truth-telling formed in Eleanor's mind the very premise and promise of Danny K.M.'s character, a container for her growing col- lection of ideas about him.

This time she clicked "Images" and a single photo tagged with his name appeared at the top of the screen above a mass of other photos—a fighter jet, a wasted woman in a beaded gown, two butter- flies perched on a branch—proposed as close matches by Google's unfathomable algorithm. The picture was low-res and taken in dim light, apparently on a dance floor, though closer inspection revealed its resemblance to a gym. The man tagged in the image was locked in a nontrivial maneuver with a woman in shorts and heels whose head, which led her torso in an acrobatic backward arch, was cut off by the left edge of the frame. A click on "View page" led to a blog called Kizomba Senga Adore, a fan site for a kind of music and accompanying dance style that were unfamiliar to Eleanor but which she quickly learned were variations on the Angolan folk tradition that had been taken up recently—especially kizomba, the newer iteration of the two—as forms of dirty dancing (this allusion was not Eleanor's but the site's) in clubs across both hemispheres.

What we know about dirty dancing: Some time after Abraham had left but before the rest of her relationships had been reduced to the exchange of texts, Eleanor had streamed the 1987 movie on her new laptop after hearing its theme song—"[I've Had] The Time of My Life"—blare from the window of a passing Prius. Streaming *Dirty Dancing* led her to stream *All That Heaven Allows*, which led her to stream *Ali: Fear Eats the Soul*. She did not stream *Far from Heaven* because she had seen it not long before in the Todd Haynes retrospective at the Cinemathèque. She had thought about the relation of these films to class and race, but she had not thought about the relation of them to her interest in Danny K.M. She had thought about how the centrality of the relationship of female aging to desire in three of the films relates to the more standard coming-of-age narrative in the fourth, but she had not thought of this in terms of the effect of time on her own aging cells. When *Ali: Fear Eats the Soul* was released in 1974, the lead actress, Brigitte Mira, was sixty-four years old. Eleanor was now thirty-nine. Patrick Swayze, the muscled star of *Dirty Dancing*—a sleeper hit worth more than $200 million and counting—died in 2009 at fifty-seven after a battle with pancreatic cancer waged in the public eye. In that film's B story—it's set in 1963—a working-class white dancer's botched back-alley abortion is fixed by the doctor-father of the Jewish ingénue, Baby, who has to confront her class privilege before earning the dancer's gratitude. In the A story, Baby discovers her sexuality on an integrated staff dance floor. In both the A and B stories, the women are caught by the men.

No further information could be gleaned about Danny from Kizomba Senga Adore. Eleanor sent the photo to her housemates' Epson and, holding the printout at arm's length, trimmed off all but Danny's face. In black and white, pixilated and in profile, the specifics of his features were hard to make out. He looked young, but out of his teens. His skin was dark and his face was round. He seemed self-conscious about dancing, or about having his photo taken while dancing.

She slid the postage stamp–sized photo into her wallet, behind her newly activated Visa, and typed on her phone:

> Hi Danny,
> I thought maybe we could meet this afternoon and you could give me the DVDs, whatever you've managed to copy. I'll be at the coffee place on 4th and President, the one with the sandwich board outside and no windows to the street. I'll be there from 12:00 to 2:00. My skin is pale. I'm wearing a light-brown dress. My hair is brown.
> Eleanor

It was 9:30 when she left the apartment. The humidity had caught up to the heat, and as Eleanor wove through the partially blocked sidewalks that bordered construction sites for more new high-rises, she felt her dress cling to the backs and insides of her thighs. She'd proposed a meeting at the café where her laptop had disappeared because of her ambivalence about encountering Danny, an ambivalence that shifted sharply from one pole to the other based on the unknown variable of his guilt. A quick search on her phone while she walked confirmed that, indeed, the cliché about people returning to the scenes of their crimes was reinforced by the U.S. government, which claims in its FBI *Crime Classification Manual* that at least "disorganized" serial killers—those "more susceptible to feelings of fear or regret"—are likely to haunt the sites of their deeds. If Danny K.M. *was* a classifiable criminal, Eleanor reasoned, he would count as a "disorganized" one. What could have motivated him to contact her other than some kind of feeling—of regret, or fear of cosmic retribution?

The lenses of her sunglasses weren't sufficiently dark and she squinted behind them, feeling the wrinkles that fanned from her eyes grow deeper. Five or six workers in hard hats, all men, younger than Eleanor and of varied ethnicities, stood in a clump on the corner ahead, peeling cellophane off sandwiches and popping the lids on cans of soda. She would have to pass within ten feet of them or conspicuously cross the street—she was the only pedestrian on her stretch of sidewalk—and she braced herself for the catcalls, comments, overt or covert once-overs. She pulled the fabric of her dress from her legs, but the separation and modesty afforded by this gesture lasted only a few steps.

It was possible, of course, that the interaction she'd come to expect from years of walking through cities as a woman alone, a woman with pale skin and brown hair who was neither obese nor undernourished, who could breathe on her own and without the help of some machine, would not reproduce itself this time. That the uninvited attention she got from men was usually of the ostensibly genial kind rather than the ostensibly hostile kind, and that the corollary of this generality—when she did want attention, she was able to obtain it—could, and often did, translate into material advantage had felt like a dull and immutable fact of Eleanor's life. She could deny neither its injustice nor its use-value; she could rail against it but she could not get outside of it completely. It was surely a cause of the shame she experienced—though often unnoticed—as a kind of vibration undergirding her every move, like a refrigerator's hum. It made her wary of nearly all male attention and, as an extension, of male authority and authority in general, which had set her on a path of, among other things, academic failure, self- and under-employment, and a fierce loyalty to the women in her life. But so many of those women, whom she'd thought to be just like her—to think just like her, as best friends assume to be the case when they're young and waiting together for their lives to begin—turned out to be just slightly not like her, and those slight differences had led, over the years, to more consequential differences, until the moment when she discovered—this may be related, she thought now, to the thing that had happened, that she had made or let happen—that the women to whom she was so fiercely loyal had made choices that were in fact fundamentally different, especially in relation to male authority and to authority in general, from hers, and that even though their mutual fierce loyalty might well continue in the face of this difference, it was a difference nonetheless, and one that contrib-uted to Eleanor's feeling of special loneliness in this moment, as she walked somewhat quickly by five or six male road workers, humid in her dress, attempting both to ignore and to interpret the expres-sions on their faces.

This time—and an objective observer would have noted that this was becoming gradually more common—there were no catcalls, no overtures attempting to intimidate or to charm; but then one of the men said Have a good afternoon to Eleanor's back. Good after-noon, said Eleanor under her breath, relieved, then doubting the basis for her relief.

Emmi Kurowski, the house-cleaning heroine from *Ali: Fear Eats the Soul*, is desired by Ali (many years her junior) but by no one else.

Gena Rowlands was forty-seven when *Opening Night* premiered in 1977, likely forty-six at the time of filming; Susan Sarandon was forty-five when she played Louise and is now, at near seventy, still called "steamy" in the press. Eleanor had heard her great-aunt Iphigenia, once undeniably beautiful in a conventional way, explain that the erotic attention comes earlier and lasts longer than you expect, until one day you realize it has stopped altogether.

She walked several long blocks up the shallow slope toward the park, pausing to buy a bottle of water imported from Fiji from a man glued to a televised soccer match behind the counter of an un-air-conditioned, cramped bodega. She could see up ahead the peaked white tents of the farmers' market, where on Wednesdays and Saturdays, especially in summer, the beautiful people turned out with their bikes and strollers, their scooters—the foot-powered kind and the gas-powered kind and sometimes the electric kind— and retro plaid rolling carts, to meet the producers of their organic and humanely raised food. On this particular Wednesday there was also, to the side of the market's main entrance, a small stand set up by the local SPCA with a sign inviting passersby to ADOPT A FRIEND FOR LIFE. Eleanor accepted a flyer from one of the preteens staffing the booth, then immediately threw it out.

Time passed. Eleanor tasted, sipped, met her producers.

She sat on her book bag on the grass, ate a veggie tamale from the food truck, paged through a copy of the free weekly that someone had left for trash. There was a story in it about an indie-rock band that had been on the verge of crossing over with its first six albums finally gaining traction in the mainstream with the seventh. She studied the picture of the band, a full-color spread in which four men in early middle age, with slight paunches and lines fanning from their eyes like hers, posed stiffly on a rooftop against the city skyline, staring bleakly at the camera as if it might steal something from them.

Time passed. Eleanor walked. At 11:55, she entered the wood-lined coffee shop to which she had not returned since the wintry afternoon that now seemed so long ago, though fewer than twelve weeks had gone by. The plywood in the windows had been replaced by glass, bright beams of dust-trapping light transforming the atmosphere of the place. She ordered a macchiato, installed herself at the same table she'd been sitting at on the day of the theft, and opened up *Artificial Hells: Participatory Art and the Politics of Spectatorship*, a book she had not yet begun reading, that she had ordered impulsively after hearing it described in conversation as being critical of the idealization of collaboration and pessimistic about the political potential of art. It was the kind of drunken online purchase she made sometimes late at night amid a surge of active curiosity about her future, an emergent uprising of the question she spent most of her time suppressing: What, if anything, can I do in the time I have left?

Artificial Hells was a thick book, and Eleanor began with the illustrations. There were pictures of *Total Participation (1966)* by El Groupo de los Artes de los Medios Masivos and of *120 Minutes Dedicated to the Divine Marquis (1965)* by Jean-Jacques Lebel; pictures with captions like "View of the container" or "Installation view . . . after being destroyed." The picture of a woman washing her crotch with a rag made Eleanor think of a Degas pastel she had stared at for an afternoon once at the Met, the folded pose of the model as she bent over her washing cloth and tub expressing—

simultaneously and incongruously—fatigue, stability, and submission. The picture of the skinny 1970s bodies in *To Exorcise the Spirit of Catastrophe* made her think of the hunger strike in an Israeli jail that she'd read about that morning, in which two Palestinian political prisoners being held without charge had refused meals for close to three months in a performance the intended audience for which was also the commissioning body.

The pictures and the titles and the tangents they led to occupied Eleanor's attention in exactly the right way for someone whose purpose sitting in a café and nursing a macchiato was not to be reading a book but to be waiting for the appearance within a two-hour window of a person whose identity might not be easy to verify and who, in all likelihood, would not show up at all.

Time passed. Having taken in all the information she could glean from the pictures and their captions, and feeling already too full of information to consider reading a word of the text itself, she saw that it was 2:00. Danny K.M. had not come. Her retroactive recognition of the inevitability of this outcome caused the heat of a private embarrassment to perforate her skin. She uncrossed her legs—still slick with sweat—put away her book, got up, bussed her table, and walked into the heat and sun, squinting from the moment she opened the door.

WE HAD NOT BEEN in contact for nearly two weeks, but I couldn't reclaim the space the critic had come to occupy in my mind. He had not stopped emailing just because I stopped responding. I saved his messages, unread, in a folder labeled "*".

It required discipline not to open his messages, but I was afraid of what reading them might do to the revision. His credentials as a reviewer and the author of three influential books, along with his innate—and/or inherited, and/or developed—confidence, meant that the critic had from the beginning assumed the position of power in our literary discussions. It was not so much the fact of this but the way the fact of it seemed natural that enraged me, once I'd granted myself space to think. Other points of connection between us—common interests; my genuine concern for his physical and psychic well-being and my equally genuine curiosity about how the uncovering of a traumatizing origin story might affect a person living in the public eye, especially one already anxious about that eye and his changing role before it—were so contaminated by the master-pupil dynamic they'd lost their purchase. Of course all of this movement and stagnation, this battle, was occurring in me alone, a civil war in which I was commander of both sides.

The Ukrainian folk style bilij holos—"white voice"—exploits the chest register and is akin to controlled screaming. When I got the urge to correspond with the critic, I would stream recordings of it on YouTube. My favorite was a song called "Hilka - Ne hody y, ulane." On the screen a static misty mountain scene.

You could say that I was becoming blurred at my edges. When I worked on my revision, the critic's marginalia invaded my mind.

Limerent bonds are characterized by "entropy" crystallization, as described by Stendhal in *On Love.* The new troubles in Crimea had yet to begin. Some listeners describe bilij holos as just shrieking.

THE TEXT MESSAGE CAME from an unknown number, minutes after Eleanor had left the café. She read:

SORRY I CAN'T COME. I'M IN
ALBANY NOW I NEVER GOT
THE DVDS NO MONEY SO
I'M SORRY AGAIN
BLESSINGS,, DANNY

She let her pace slow as she reviewed her options, holding each gingerly in her imagination for one second, two seconds, before dropping it for its competition. This toggling occupied her mind to such a degree that her body (what we know about Eleanor: she is subject to binaries) took charge of its own operations and delivered her, less than an hour later, to her building's front door.

She went upstairs and packed an overnight bag, wrote a note for her housemates, and locked the door to her room, hesitating for a moment before leaving the key in the lock.

An hour later she was at Penn Station, buying a ticket from an automated kiosk.

An hour later she was eating bibimbap at one of the Korean restaurants on Thirty-Fifth.

An hour after that she was boarding the train at gate 5E, and two hours after that she woke to the sound of the conductor brushing past and chanting the name of her destination, the station stop before Albany, in a partly gentrified town where she had a friend to whom she'd texted news of her arrival after boarding the train.

As she got up and recuperated her bag from the overhead rack, she took in the view of the summer river outside, the summer trees and summer sailboats, the summer-sunset sky, a midtoned blue slashed by orange and white that looked different outside the city, though the colors and their arrangement were the same; then, turning to the opposite side of the train as it pulled into the station, she took in the view of the summer people outside, in their summer dresses and summer sandals, their summer smiles spread across their sun-kissed summer faces.

While the other descending passengers greeted and embraced and climbed into cars and taxis, Eleanor walked the three blocks to her friend's apartment, where she would spend the night despite the fact that her friend, who was recently divorced and dating a man about whom she was ambivalent, would be out for the night. Eleanor let herself in with the key she'd been instructed to retrieve from behind a potted jade, lay down in her clothes on the lower bunk in the room of her friend's kids, who were with their father for the week, took out her Pocket Rocket and made quick use of it—aided by a mental image of the sun-kissed summer faces—then fell, as evening fell, into a dreamless sleep.

She woke and looked at her phone: 11:07. Her friend wouldn't be home for hours. She woke, as she often did, wanting bodies around her. She grabbed her wallet and her phone and *Artificial Hells* and walked to the nearest bar—also a bookstore—a place she'd been once or twice before, where she correctly assumed there would be bodies on a night like this.

Is it necessary to note that Eleanor is the type who is capable of both intense solitude and intense sociability? Usually it was clear which tendency governed a given moment, and the extent of her satisfaction or discomfort in a situation was often tethered to the extent to which her need for one or the other extreme was being met. But at this moment, in the gentrified summery bar in the partly gentrified summery upriver town, Eleanor felt the stirrings of a different desire, not unlike the feeling she'd experienced while being ejected from the artist's performance at which the young woman had been moved to take off her dress, and not unlike the feeling she'd experienced in Abraham's apartment the day she decided to read her cards, but not completely like either of those feelings either.

As she sipped her locally brewed stout and flipped through the pages of Claire Bishop's book, she was not in fact reading the book's ample text but was trying, rather, to identify the new and unfamiliar desire, which fell outside of the solitude/sociability binary, that now flowed through her body, collecting especially between her elbows and the tips of her fingers. In what she had taken to be a dreamless sleep she had in fact had a dream, an image more than a dream, of a narrow ring being tattooed around her left forearm, just below the elbow.

She rubbed her left forearm with her right hand. While she had come out for the bodies, for the bodies of other people, of strangers, while she had come out to be near them and to sense their sociality, once she found herself amid them she retreated into her own body, fled to that other pole, and she wondered what it was about her that made her crave this being-alone without being alone, this being-alone as a way of being-with. The bodies around her now, of which she finally began to take note, were not uniform in appearance or attitude: There were slim ones covered in too-loose clothing and larger ones covered in too-tight clothing; there were effortlessly elegant ones and proudly overdetermined ones; there were countless forearm tattoos. There was enough of an urban sensibility in the town that she felt as anonymous as she did in the city, even more so because her expectations of the town were different from her expectations of the city. She ran her hand through her hair; a crinkled gray strand appeared in her fingers, followed by a sudden need to be noticed, but only just, only for a minute.

But nobody noticed Eleanor. She had a powerful intuition that she might actually disappear. A line from her lost paragraphs came to mind and she recited it silently to herself: *Like a halo of death around each and every head that had the misfortune of being attached to a body.*

When a text came in of a picture of the outside of a Tim Hortons, she understood it to be telling her that Abraham had made it to Canada, that he had survived the first portion of his trip, and she was happy to see from the way the sky looked in the picture that the weather was fine in Quebec. Abraham was texting her, which meant he was thinking about her at that moment—although the photo, with its blue sky, must have been taken earlier, during the day.

Did she miss Abraham? There were certain things about him that she did miss, but which things were they? She may have missed the way he both knew her and didn't know her, and the fact that he refused categorically to promise anything he couldn't deliver. But she did not miss the missing of those things that, as a result of or indication of his refusing to promise them, he was not able to deliver—even or especially if she couldn't identify just what those things were.

Another text came in, this one containing only a bit.ly address and a signature: "XO A."

The link led to a ride report on the mobile version of a site called advrider.com, which she knew from Abraham's obsession with it stood for "adventure rider" and hosted a community of motorcycle enthusiasts who undertook long, often international trips, alone or in pairs or small groups, a community of (mostly, but not exclusively) men who nurtured inexhaustible appetites for riding into the night in all sorts of weather, camping on the sides of roads and eating reconstituted freeze-dried food out of bags using utensils un-nested from Leathermans. At the top of the ride report—beneath the title, "TLH"—was a snapshot of opened boxes filled with crumpled fabric and metal bits and jugs of something all scattered on a parquet floor, followed by several paragraphs of text:

My setup was decent for touring but I wanted a better one, so to the GIVI racks I already had I added Wolfman Expedition Dry panniers. I installed a CJ Designs tail rack with Rotopax mount and a two-gallon gas can for that 260-mile stretch from Goose Bay to Port Hope Simpson. And on top of the Rotopax went the Twisted Throttle DrySpec tail luggage system, which complements the Wolfman panniers perfectly. All my crap fit in the luggage nicely, complemented by the Oxford four-strap tank bag I'd already bought years ago to hold my camera and other quick-access stuff.

This was a language in which Abraham was fluent, and she felt sad for not taking an interest in it before. A pair of women wearing vintage '60s eyeglasses and straight-cut bangs carried pints of amber beer to the table next to hers; one of the women jostled her elbow as she sat, then smiled an apology. Eleanor nodded and kept reading:

I mounted an IRC TR8 *front tire and a Full Bore M-40 rear—the* IRC *is very similar to a* TKC-80 *in the 90/90-21 size, but the tread is spaced ever so slightly wider, and the tire costs about half of what the* TKC *does; and the Full Bore rear, while similar to a Shinko 705, also has slightly wider-spaced tread lugs and wears a lot better than the Shinko, yet works far better off pavement than it looks like it should. I debated getting a rear* TKC-80 *or Heidenau K60, but the Full Bore is literally half the price, and considering the gravel would only account for about 15% of my trip, I settled on the Full Bore as the most sensible choice.*

She could not decipher what she was reading, and only when she saw the second photo, which appeared below the text, a photo she finally understood to be of Abraham's motorcycle—though it was all but unrecognizable beneath the Twisted Throttle DrySpec tail luggage system and the IRC TR8 and the Full Bore M-40 rear— parked by the curb of what she now understood to be Abraham's street, did it become clear that this was Abraham's own ride report, the beginning of his adventure. She thought of the first time he'd mentioned this trip long ago, when for all the usual reasons, mostly money, it had seemed impossible. She was moved: something had broken; something had been broken through.

When her head hit the pink princess pillow on the lower bunk in her friend's kids' room, Eleanor could feel the accumulated sensations of her night out—the desirous loneliness and the ambivalent longing, the unexpected alienation and familiar anonymity—seep out of her head and her slowly graying hair and her sticky legs and her sore feet, out of her chest cavity and her back and her tattoo-free forearms, and disappear into the pink princess sheets, or into some quieter, less tangible place, as defended from the aggressions of the present tense as was the now-still Rocket, tucked into her bag in its pink protective sheath.

"WHAT I WANT TO SAY," I typed to the critic, "is that when Eleanor sleeps, the rearrangement of her mind's furniture happens without her direction, and often without her recall in the morning; but when she does recall, in glimpses, the results of these acts of redecoration, she becomes aware that the rearrangement has taken place not on the level of things exchanging positions in a room, but on the level of molecules and atoms changing position in the things, so that the things—the furniture, whether object, thought, or emotion—have themselves become unfamiliar, that they are in effect strokes of genius, sui generis acts of the imagination: that they are novel.

"Eleanor once learned—in college, no doubt—to see this becoming-unfamiliar as a state of breakdown, an interruption of fluency or flow (the status quo). Maybe that was Heidegger. And then she learned to appreciate the value of such an interruption: maybe that was Kristeva, or Thiong'o—she isn't sure herself. Her unsureness is part of what makes her suffer, by supporting a flawed belief that her reality—by which I mean the interpretation of conditions, not the conditions themselves—is only superficially transformable. A belief that in fundamental ways her reality (by which I mean her *right* to her reality) is constrained.

"But this is the work, isn't it? Asymmetrically, but for us all?"

I was writing to the critic after finally opening his emails. Work on my revision had been going acceptably for a stretch of nights-and-weekends, and I was suddenly worried about his well-being. Nothing had changed in my understanding of our dynamic, but a minor shift in my perception of my own abilities had allowed for my concern—which belonged to the part of our friendship that was laid on equal ground—to rise above the rest.

Before writing to him, I read through the messages in the folder labeled "*".

June 6, 11:30 p.m.:

When you told me that you like to fall asleep in public, I couldn't remember the term "martymachlia" and called you an exhibitionist; but in fact there's no technical term for what you are. The first mention of flashing in Western literature is in Herodotus, and it is, interestingly, woman-on-woman—the context was provincial humiliation staged as sexual superiority. If I discover something I can't live with, there will be decisions to be made. My celebrity is not the celebrity of David Foster Wallace or Amy Winehouse, but it is more than the celebrity I enjoyed only last year—though "enjoyed" is not the most applicable term, and I'm not quite sure what "I" it is that is supposedly doing the enjoying. Or the decision-making, for that matter.

June 8, 6:00 a.m.:

time passed time passed time passed time passed time passed time passed time passed time passed time past time past time passed time passed time past time passed time passed time

passed time passed time passed time passed time passed time
passed time passed time past time past time passed time passed
time past time passed time pssst time passed time passed time
passed time passed time passed time passed time passed time
passed time passed time past time past time passed time passed
time past time passed time passed time passed time passed
time pssst time passed time passed time passed time passed
time passed time past time past time passed time passed time
past time passed time passed time passed time passed time
passed time passed time passed time passed time passed time
past time past time passed time pssst passed time past time
passed time passed time passed time passed time passed time
passed time passed time passed time passed time past time past
time passed time passed time past time passed time passed
time passed time passed time passed time passed time passed
time passed time passed time past time time passed time passed
time passed time passed time passed time passed time passed
time passed time past time past time passed time passed time
past time passed time passed time passed time passed time
passed time passed time passed time passed time passed time
past time past time passed time passed time past time passed
time pssst time passed time passed time passed time passed
time passed time passed time passed time passed time passed
time past time past time passed time passed time past time
passed time passed time passed time passed time pssst time
passed time passed time passed time passed time passed time
past time past time passed time passed time past time passed
time passed time passed time passed time passed time passed
time passed time passed time passed time past time past time
passed time pssst passed time past time passed time passed
time passed time passed time passed time passed time passed
time passed time passed time past time past time passed time

passed time past time passed time passed time passed time
passed time passed time passed time passed time passed time
passed time past time time passed time passed time passed
time passed time passed time passed time passed time passed
time past time past time passed time passed time past time
passed time passed time passed time passed time passed time
passed time passed time passed time passed time past time past
time passed time passed time past time passed time pssst time
passed time passed time passed time passed time passed time
passed time passed time passed time passed time past time past
time passed time passed time past time passed time passed
time passed time passed time pssst time passed time passed
time passed time passed time passed time past time past time
passed time passed time past time passed time passed time
passed time passed time passed time passed time passed time
passed time passed time past time past time passed time pssst
passed time past time passed time passed time passed time
passed time passed time passed time passed time passed time
passed time past time

I think this is what you really want to write.

June 11, 2:13 p.m.:

Here is a portrait of me posing with the panelists at the
Norwegian premiere. Note that the crowd is small. The film
was subtitled. There are no accurate data about the number
of speakers of Norwegian currently alive on our planet. The
Norwegian word for cigarette is *sigarett*. The word for play is
teaterstykke. There is no word for please; instead of pardon they
say *flytt deg!* which means "move yourself!" My handler had her
baby, three weeks early. Everybody is fine. I haven't called my

mother or heard from Laurance. I know not the status of the cube of ice. The word for pregnant is *gravid*. The word for sick is *syk*. I have forgotten several of my English words and am counting on you to restore them. The word for home is *hjem*. I'll be hjem soon.

I felt instinctively that his mention of famous-artist suicides was a drunken flourish rather than an actual threat that required intervention, but still it seemed that responding to his correspondence was the right thing to do. I decided to leave his messages alone and started a new thread about my revision in which I typed everything I wanted to say about it to the critic.

"Is there a way out of this misunderstanding—the passivity it breeds?" I typed.

"What I want to say is that Eleanor doesn't know."

ELEANOR BREAKFASTED with her friend and listened to her recount the story of the previous night's date, during which the friend had confessed her ambivalent feelings to the man who had invited her as his guest to an extravagant dinner of locally slaughtered meats at a restaurant he knew she couldn't afford. Since the confession came just as they were finishing their entrées, the man had asked the friend if she wanted to "treat him" to coffee and dessert, betraying (in the friend's words) the contingencies of his chivalry: his voice had quivered as he pronounced "dessert." Eleanor and her friend laughed, but there was a vertigo to their laughter that nauseated Eleanor, and as truly fond as she was of her friend— as truly fond as she was of all her friends—she was relieved when it was time to pack up her overnight bag and walk the three blocks to the train station to catch the 12:17 north to Albany, where she had called ahead to reserve a spot in a semi-private room at the city's only surviving youth hostel.

When she emerged at the Albany-Rensselaer stop, she consulted her phone: the hostel was 6.2 miles away. Unwilling to navigate an unfamiliar, perhaps nonexistent system of public transport or to spend money on a cab, she set out on foot: first across the river, then along an interminable stretch of Central Avenue. Her overnight bag pulled at her right shoulder, and she could feel the sun burn her forehead, deepening the horizontal creases she had first noticed beginning to develop years ago but that she had only recently started to recognize as the onset of inevitable corporeal decline.

"Sure, you look older now than when we met," Abraham had said when she expressed her concern about the appearance of the lines. She'd conducted erratic searches for holistic remedies and natural collagen simulators; her favorite came from a site called faceyogamethod.com, which promoted a simple technique of controlled squinting as a free DIY alternative to Botox. Now, marching slowly down the broad treeless avenue—devoid also of pedestrians or open businesses—she began to perform the exercises.

1) Encircling your eyes and brows with your thumbs and forefingers, press hard into your forehead.

2) Open your eyes wide, then squint, then open, then squint, keeping your brows and forehead stationary, until you feel the years melt away and your youthful vitality return.

Eleanor's youthful vitality did not return, but she did find that intermittent repetition of the movements made the time pass more quickly, and soon she had reached her halfway point, the Honest Weight Food Co-op. She went in and ate lunch in its small windowless café, something made with quinoa and vegetables and no discernible salt.

The hostel was in a run-down three-story brick building on Swan Street, directly across from a concrete monolith that, from the signage, apparently housed the bulk of the state government. She imagined that when it was erected, a row of houses identical to the one that contained this one had been razed. The hostel was on the lucky side of the street.

The manager, a giant man with a sunburned bald head and vintage corduroy suit who introduced himself too loudly as Ross, greeted her from the stoop. All she wanted was to lie down.

Ross: Só! You've come to Albany on fóot! From whence do you háil?

Eleanor: Oh, I've only come from the Amtrak on foot. I don't have a sleep sack. Do you sell those?

Ross: Almost all the way from Troy, then! My journey began in Cánada, not nearly as auspícious, eh? Yés we have sleep sacks. How long have you been on the róad?

Eleanor: I'm not sure I'm on a road . . .

She had no notion of how to finish her sentence. This did not deter Ross.

Ross: You are on the páth! Which is not the same thíng as a road. Bureaucracy, meetings, engineers, eminent domáin—nothing good in a road. But a páth—you can cut a path through almost ánything—

Besides his accent, Ross had a way of speaking that incorporated stress on certain words and syllables, not always corresponding to their importance but imparting a musical cadence to his sentences that Eleanor might have found charming were she not so enervated from her walk.

Eleanor (valiantly): Sleep sack?

Ross (extracting a plastic-wrapped sleep sack from somewhere behind the counter): We have to remember the difference between wándering and being lóst. Twelve dollars. Room number 8. You're sharing with someone named Dévin, provided he gets here before eleven. We close at eleven.

Ross's hyperstimulated affect had almost normalized by the end of his last sentence, and Eleanor smiled, handed him her card, signed the slip, and trudged upstairs to room number 8.

That morning, before she had left for the train, Eleanor's friend had asked her over breakfast what in the hell she thought she was doing. Eleanor had responded, Well what are you doing? I don't know, said the friend. Midlife crisis? Maybe this is what that looks like, said Eleanor. Maybe it is, said the friend, and there was silence.

But seriously, Eleanor, said the friend after the silence, what are you doing, going to godforsaken Albany to stay in a youth hostel and hunt down someone whose character is unknown to you, who may or may not be in possession of your data and who won't tell you how to find him? Eleanor had no answer. All she knew was that she was going to godforsaken Albany, at least in part, to do those things.

Her fantasies about Danny K.M. weren't usually sexual. She imagined talking to him about his past and his future, their conversation lubricated by the alcoholic drink of his choice. She imagined interviewing him about his job skills and helping him with his résumé, something she was trained to do for others, though she largely failed on her own behalf. She imagined, once or twice, telling him about the thing that had happened. She wanted to expose herself to Danny K.M.—the way the girl in the summery dress had wanted to expose herself to the artist. She wanted to meet his gesture of what she took to be frank generosity with her own equally frank gesture. But she wanted all of this while simultaneously not wanting it, or more accurately, while wanting the buffer of a margin (of what kind, she didn't know) around whatever encounter might eventually occur. In this sense, her fantasies did not belong to the romance of novels with covers featuring mustachioed lotharios, but to something less singular—part maternal care, part Romantic Sublime.

She was proactive: She sent emails and texts to Danny directly, to which he did not reply. She discovered a nongovernmental organization that managed the resettlement of asylum seekers in the area and offered aid to other immigrants with limited resources, including legal help, language instruction, and a job placement service that, thanks to budgetary rules or just the economy, was forced to sacrifice fit for immediacy. She learned that some of those being resettled were from Eastern Africa. Her assumption that Danny K.M. might be from that region and in those circumstances was founded, hastily and tentatively, on a handful of details including an internet search on his family name, his pixilated appearance in the dancing photo, his allusions in their correspondence to being newly arrived and without money, and the fact that he had traveled from the state's cultural capital, which did not house resettlement offices, to its administrative capital, which did. She called the organization to ask if it were possible to locate a recent arrival by name, but the receptionist told her that data was not public and invited Eleanor to attend the next orientation for volunteers in two months' time.

She spent her afternoons doing "research" from one of the few Wi-Fi cafés on a three-block stretch of Lark Street, the neighborhood that felt the most like an imperfect clone of similar streets in the city and in her friend's town: strings of storefronts that had been transformed in performatively organic and then shamelessly mercenary ways to attract just the kind of customer Eleanor—with her laptop and smartphone and boots, with her self-conscious melancholy— was. Half expecting Danny K.M. to walk into the café she had chosen on a given afternoon, she would sit within view of the door so that she could look up whenever someone entered and compare the face of the newcomer with her mental image of the snapshot of Danny that remained undisturbed, tucked into her wallet behind her Visa. It seemed Albany did not teem with the kind of customer Eleanor was; no matter which café she chose, she rarely had occasion to look up.

On what would turn out to be her last day in town, but before she knew that to be the case, Eleanor was sitting in her usual spot at the Muddy Cup, laptop closed on the table in front of her, mood poisoned by the futility of the afternoon's research and a creeping anxiety about money, triggered by the arrival of her credit card bill to her in-box, then duly compartmentalized by way of another one-click minimum payment. She heard the door open and looked up: Danny K.M. entered, followed immediately by Ross, who had to duck to fit through the door of the basement-level café. Danny, in denim and white canvas sneakers, walked to the counter to order. Ross walked to Eleanor's table and hovered, or loomed.

"Hel-ló!" Ross said to Eleanor.

"Hel-ló," Eleanor said, her heart invading her throat.

ELEANOR TRIED TO FOCUS on Ross, who had been only kind to her in her time at the hostel, keeping the promise he'd made once Devin failed to show that first night to let her stay alone in the semi-private room.

"Are you fine?" Ross asked, his head tilting down and to the left, eyes in a slight squint.

"I'm fine," said Eleanor, smiling wide. "Do I look not-fine?"

By pretending to crack her back in a yoga-like maneuver she would not normally perform, she was able to catch a glimpse of Danny K.M. as he sat down at a small table just behind hers and picked up a magazine some previous customer had abandoned.

"I always ask people if they're fíne or nót because they're more likely to tell me the trúth that way, whereas nobody really héars you when you ask them How áre you?—"

Ross pulled back the chair opposite Eleanor and sat.

"—How áre you isn't even a quéstion anymore, it's like a bránd náme, you know, when the méaning has been effectively drained oút of the words, leaving behind only sóunds . . . like Chéerio! or Twisted Síster or Nirvána—I álways forget what that's called!" Ross grinned as he spoke.

"I forget too," said Eleanor. "But I'm really fine. I'm just finishing up with my work."

Pretending to be scratching her ankle, she reached down and extracted her phone from her bag, then placed it on her right thigh, keeping her eyes, as much as was possible, on Ross.

"How well do you know the Hudson River?" asked Ross, his tone dropping momentarily both in volume and in eccentricity.

Eleanor said, "Huh?" glancing down to type her pass code and click "Contacts."

"The Húdson Ríver." He leaned in. "This fláwed, majéstíc vein, which on the second Thursday of every month, well of every súmmer month, is the site of a cítywíde—Oh! Stein!"

A used copy of *Composition as Explanation,* which she'd picked up at the bookstore-bar, sat closed on her table.

"I find her unbéarable as a persona," he went on, "Excépt! Excépt for the recordings of her magnificent voíce! Have you ever heard—"

Ross didn't wait for Eleanor to tell him that she had, in fact, heard several recordings of Gertrude Stein reading, that she played one routinely during the ekphrasis unit when she taught composition, although that had become less frequent as she climbed the so-called adjunct ladder. She couldn't take in, let alone engage, Ross's ambivalence about Stein or the fact that this ambivalence was a sentiment they shared. She could feel Danny K.M.'s presence behind her, could hear him sipping his iced drink through a straw, flipping pages, she imagined, in his magazine.

"Móst people like her recording of the 'Pórtrait of Picásso,' which is obviously gréat, but there are bétter ones, like 'Matísse'—and the bits from *The Máking of Américans,* which are my fávorite . . ."

Eleanor nodded. It was "Picasso" that she had played to her class. Ross fell silent for a moment, and she tried again, this time successfully, to call up the Contacts screen on her phone.

"Eleanor," said Ross, "Can I ask you something?"

"Sure," said Eleanor, blindly thumb-typing "Da" into the search bar.

Ross paused for a few seconds, and then:

"Eleanor, would you dáte a guy like me? I mean, if I asked you to go on a dáte, like to go to second Thursdays with me, ás my date, would you say yes, or would you even say máybe? Or would you say nó, because I'm just not the kind of guy that you would want to dáte, even though you probably think I'm an o.k. gúy, but just not someone you think of ín thát wáy, right? I mean, that's what you would say, isn't it?"

Eleanor looked at Ross, but he had turned away. She looked down and thumb-typed "Muddy Cup?" She looked up at Ross, who had turned back toward her with a closed-lipped smile and humid eyes. She hit "Send" without looking, and a *joop!* rose from her thigh. "Excuse me," Ross said and pushed back his chair. The espresso machine wailed. She heard no ping or vibration from Danny K.M.'s phone, but the screech of chair legs or the wail of the machine might have been covering one up. Ross stood behind a young couple waiting in line at the counter, holding hands. Eleanor pried her attention from Danny and tried to think of a response to Ross's question, a response she felt he deserved. He was kind and considerate; he was knowledgeable and he listened; his clothing and lifestyle indicated an immunity to consumerism that she ought to have admired, and did, though she also suspected that something of a reaction formation was at play in the quaint clothing and belabored pattern of speech.

He was probably two decades her senior, or close. She thought of saying, But what about that nice age-appropriate lady over there? She thought of saying, We all hope someone else's youth will rub off on us. She thought of saying no to his invitation, and she thought of saying yes. She might have thought of Emmi and Ali from Fassbinder's film, but then Ross was standing over her, holding a to-go cup of coffee and pulling crumbling morsels of scone from a waxed-paper bag. Eleanor wanted to tell him he shouldn't stoop, that his uprightness alone, if he would take possession of it, could attract someone who might give him what he needed. She said nothing. She heard Danny K.M. get up from the table behind her.

"Ross," said Eleanor without intention.

She knew that her time at the hostel was over, knew that she would try to repair things with Ross, whom she had come to consider a kind of friend. She knew, also, that repair would not be simple or immediate.

"I'm going to gó now," said Ross, and he did.

Danny K.M. had gotten up for a refill. Eleanor brought her hand to her neck and breathed into her pulse. With her other hand she touched the circular green icon on her screen. She turned: The flip phone on the table behind her did not vibrate or ring. Its light didn't light. The barista called out, "Iced white for Steve!" and Danny K.M., who was no longer Danny K.M. but an older man, a man at least in his thirties, a man apparently named Steve—whose resemblance to Danny K.M. was limited to the contours of his body and face in profile, his skin tone, and Eleanor's own desire—returned to his table with his iced white latte, and he nodded to Eleanor as if he often caught women staring expectantly at his phone, and Eleanor, without thinking, as something broke deep inside her, nodded back.

WHAT YOU MIGHT be thinking about Eleanor: that she is impulsive, that if she keeps going like this she will never find her way, that she would do well to move with more caution through this phase of her life, a phase that might appear on a map of her trajectory—if there were such a map, and if it could be trusted to portray her life with any degree of accuracy—as a smudge. Or: that where matters of importance are at stake, she is not nearly impulsive enough. Is it necessary to say that both judgments are equally valid, which is to say, also, that they are equally suspect? Is it necessary, furthermore, to recall that even when the events of the day temporarily overshadow it, the thing that had happened—thing-prime—and this is exacerbated by the missing paragraphs and the vanished site for a certain kind of thinking—continues to create and shed its residue on Eleanor's trajectory, like the finest dust settling on our imagined map?

Illustrations deleted from the fourth draft

1. Diagram showing points of pressure
2. Thelma and Louise flying off cliff
3. Pina Bausch's dancers: A planned not-catching
4. Mustachioed kiss: A first lesson
5. "Russians" (Sting)
6. A magnetic field, produced by moving electric charges and the intrinsic magnetic movements of elementary particles associated with a fundamental quantum property, their spin
7. Women, mirrors, tears (Gena Rowlands): Between technology and authenticity
8. Props (fake whiskey, gun)
9. Fissures lit from below
10. Calculations from the mean lifetime (table)
11. *Dirty Dancing:* The women are caught by the men
12. Degas: Fatigue, stability, submission
13. Faceyogamethod.com: Eyes open
14. Faceyogamethod.com: Squint
15. Motorcycle handlebars
16. View from ferry
17. Two bikes, one with sheepskin seat cover
18. The open road; cotton balls in the sky
19. A simple network of underground wells and tunnels (the form of a feeling)

HER NAME WAS CAROLYN, though she looked more like a River or a Calliope or a Tree. She had collected Eleanor from the bus drop-off in a new-model red pickup truck, which she drove without shoes. "Psyched to show you the fa-arm," she sang lightly, her eyes on the road.

Carolyn had glitter in her hair and glitter on her face; she wore a heavily embroidered white tunic and a faded green hoodie. She had yarn tied around her ankles, just below twin California-poppy tattoos, and she walked barefoot on the gravel paths as she led Eleanor on the "short-form" tour of Crescent Farm. Eleanor took in her host's résumé—she was born in a hamlet in western PA, held a BA from Harvard and an MA from Oxford, and had returned five months ago from a yearlong Rotary scholarship in Addis Ababa, Ethiopia—as they proceeded single file from yurt #1 (with solar power) to yurt #2 (without); from the ungainly vegetable garden to the towering compost heap; from the neat row of mail-order beehives to the roiling swimming hole; from the chicken coop to the pond.

As they walked, they encountered three of the six other full-time members of the Crescent Farm community: Sol (tall, happy, stoned); Krystal (plump and pierced, the "fairy godmother" of the compound, which Eleanor took to mean she'd had something to do with funding its construction); and Cole (buzz cut, possibly trans- or agender, smiling: "the mediator around here"). Eleanor should not have been surprised to see people who looked like punks and people who looked like hippies living together in a cutting-edge eco squat; it had been a long time, she knew, since fashion was a reliable marker for anything. The residents all appeared to be in their late twenties or thereabouts. The other three members, Carolyn explained to Eleanor, were inside the main house preparing dinner. 'Couchsurfer's *Spe-cia-le*,' she sang, flicking a sparkly fingernail against Eleanor's arm.

Set back a quarter of a mile from the road and the small gravel pad where Carolyn had parked the truck, the main house sat in isolation in a clearing, oriented toward the south to maximize solar gain. A mountain of grass-covered earth ("man-made thermal mass," chanted Carolyn) hugged the length of its north face. Approaching from the south, the two women were greeted by a wall of windows at least fifty feet long and twenty feet high. Carolyn gestured across the facade and spoke words that meant nothing to Eleanor: Trombe wall, spectral glazing, solar chimney, selective surface. What Eleanor saw was a sleek, modern, wood-clad house lacking the support structures that give most rural and exurban homes their sense of limitation: the strung-up power lines, propane tank, matching two-car garage.

The main room was vast, with a polished concrete floor and slanted plywood ceiling pierced by a row of tiny skylights. The living area consisted of an L-shaped sofa, a scattering of beanbags, a top-of-the-line ping-pong table, a wall of bookshelves, and a gray pit bull asleep on a white flokati rug. It was very neat. The kind of place, Eleanor thought, that would be christened "eco-minimalist" by a fawning journalist for the Style section of the *Times*. On the kitchen end, where Eleanor and Carolyn had entered, small hills of produce—radishes and baby beets, purple pod beans, symmetrical heads of lettuce and copious amounts of kale—were lined up on a long wooden counter, flanked by little piles of dirt where the roots had been jostled as the plants were set down.

The cooks were Bin (a citizen of Myanmar who'd recently graduated from Cornell), Matt (a surfer or snowboarder, probably both), and Ophelia, a stern, bespectacled woman from Ithaca who looked about eighteen and greeted Eleanor with a nod. "Any allergies?" she asked, tossing a handful of walnuts into an oblong wooden bowl. With the exception of Bin, the residents were white or appeared so, and their exposed skin showed a range of sensitivity to the sun: Ophelia's shoulders were so burned they made Eleanor wince.

The stove was manned by one of three current "shorties": short-term residents, Carolyn explained, who weren't invested in the property but who could stay for between one and three months in exchange for designated hours of labor and a weekly donation to the house fund. The shorties—but not the full-timers, for a reason that was not explained—were given nicknames. Eleanor was introduced to the one at the stove, Kicker, and he gestured to the other two, who were outside smoking, their backs visible through the expanse of glass. "They like to name visitors too," Kicker said over his shoulder. "Someone usually comes up with something during the first meal. You'll see." Eleanor wondered what Kicker had done to earn his name.

Krystal emerged from the cellar carrying four unlabeled green champagne bottles. "Last of the crop!" she announced, depositing them on the counter. The previous October, during a banner year for fruit trees, they'd made several cases' worth of hard cider from the wild apples that proliferated on the ten-acre property. Each bottle had fermented a little differently, Ophelia explained, "because we aren't interested in controlling the process with commercial yeasts or aggressive sterilization." Some were basically virgin; others were stronger than beer. Some were flat and others carbonated. Krystal opened all four bottles, distributing them across the long table, and everyone—including the smokers, whose entry was accompanied by an odor of tobacco breath and skin that triggered a sharp longing in Eleanor—sat at the table.

Eleanor had taken the empty spot next to Cole, who opened the conversation only after swallowing a pint of cider.

"So, what brings you here, Eleanor?"

"Oh, they didn't tell you?"

She had found the listing on couchsurfing.com within five minutes of deciding that she needed to flee the hostel and Ross and the specter of Danny K.M.

"No, I mean, why are you on the road?"

"Oh, I'm not really. I'm . . . trying to plan my next move."

"What kind of move?"

"I'm gathering data," Eleanor said, after a silence.

Carolyn intercepted her at the sink, where she was rinsing her glass before switching to wine, the cider supply having quickly been consumed. The bowls of fragrant food were half-empty; the smokers had gone back outside again. "Cole tells me you're looking for a place to go," Carolyn said conspiratorially. "You would absolutely love Addis, I guarantee it. I can put you in touch with some awesome folks." She touched a hand to Eleanor's arm and left it there, while Eleanor thought of the blogs satirizing voluntourists that she had discovered in her research into Danny K.M., while she wondered if Carolyn's photos could even be among those she'd seen on said blogs, photos of dust-covered orphans propped on the sturdy hips of seemingly sturdy collegiates. "Yo, Data!"—a "shortie" named Biscuit had been lurking behind them and was now yelling practically in

Eleanor's ear—"Cole christened you. Now let's get you some of this," and a lit joint was placed in her hand.

Seated across from Eleanor was the short-termer they called Vision, or Viz, not—according to Cole—because he was spiritual but because he had mentioned in passing on his first night that he had 20/15 eyesight, a diagnosis Eleanor always found confounding since it seems to describe a superpower. The first thing she noticed about Viz was that he was a regaler, one of those men in their thirties with apparently undramatic, comfortable backgrounds who have made an effort to compensate for their lack of childhood struggle by doing something daring or noble as adults, like dropping out of grad school or spending a couple of years in Jakarta writing for an English-language newspaper, and who keep themselves informed about current events and esoteric subjects alike to make it possible to hold court precisely at communal meals such as these. The second thing Eleanor noticed about Viz was that he had a very nice chest, which he flashed while removing his sweater midmeal. As the evening went on and more wine was drunk, and as night fell slowly outside the south-facing windows, as candles were lit and more joints passed around, Eleanor noticed—then felt self-conscious for noticing—the many very nice things that Viz had in addition to the chest (which she continued to picture beneath his thin checkered shirt), such as a very nice pair of hands, and a very nice tattoo of a wave form on his forearm, and a very nice full-lipped mouth, and a very nice flicker in his dark eyes—she also questioned the flicker—particularly when he looked across the table at Eleanor to approve of or take issue with her contribution to whatever debate was engaging the group.

Time passed. Viz's physical characteristics continued to draw Eleanor's body toward him while her mind fought for control of the margins of her experience, in which were inscribed a mortal fear of false consciousness along with an injunction against the belief that expressions of desire should be simple, reciprocal, and free.

The conversation turned to the question of Crescent Farm's economy, and Viz and Eleanor found themselves in frequent accord during what turned into a prolonged disagreement over whether the farm's ultimate goal should be to reject the dollar completely or, instead, to follow the example of the nearby, defunct Oneida Community, which at the time of its collapse due to interpersonal and ideological discord still managed to retain millions of dollars in assets, a nest egg the Oneida Corporation reinvested into its line of flatware.

"I think we should take Buddhist economics more seriously," said Cole.

"I am just so allergic to the word *investment*," said Krystal.

"There's nothing wrong with having a business plan," said Bin.

Viz and Eleanor were agnostic about the question of ditching the dollar, were agnostic about sustainable enterprise, social business, strategic inclusion, and radical separatism. But they shared a skepticism about the stakes of such a discussion among people who all had access, if not to savings accounts, at least to student loans and high-limit credit cards that allowed them, for now, to sit beneath twenty-foot dust-free ceilings and discuss these options; and they shared, it turned out, a suspicion that emerged during the course of the conversation, almost a belief (based partly on the historical record, partly on related personal experience), that groups like this live and die by the charisma of their leaders. Conjoined to their hunch that a sustainable, consensual, nonhierarchical society was almost certainly beyond reach was their near-total melancholy in the face of this fact, a melancholy that seemed to bind them together across the wide wood table and that blurred Eleanor at her edges, just where the structure of her feeling met the margin of her thought.

She got up, crossed the concrete floor diagonally, and opened a door marked with a cartoon sketch of Rodin's *Thinker* sitting on a bucket. She entered a room lined in cedar boards with a claw-foot tub at its center, a pedestal sink on one side, and around a corner separated from the bath area by a drop cloth curtain, a large wooden structure that resembled a throne but that, after a closer look, Eleanor determined was a composting toilet. A few fig- and patchouli-scented candles had been placed on a shelf and lit, but the odor, not exactly like that of a traditional outhouse but not exactly unlike it either, persisted. Eleanor lifted her dress and listened to the sound of her urine falling on sawdust.

THE CRITIC HAD written me a one-line email that I'd hesitated to return: "I'm back and I'd like very much to see you."

Now, a week later, I sat down to respond.

I typed, "From the margins, the text appears as an undifferentiated block. Paragraphs resemble one another. In romance novels, all the action is contained inside the block: For this reason, they are printed with almost no margin. For this reason, the decision to enter is fraught with risk. One's bearings can be lost. An anti-Sublime, or a post-Sublime: the machinery has been effaced. There is something about this entering and its fraughtness, something I sense is important to the revision. Though this is emphatically not a romance."

I typed, "I have a question for you about the title of my book."

I typed, "I would like to see you too. I would like for you to suggest a plan."

THE MIRROR BY the toilet was confusing Eleanor, and not only because her reflection was partially effaced in the candlelight. One of her eyes was now higher than the other, and her chin had lost its symmetry. But she didn't linger on her confusion. She was stoned—on top of the circulating joints, the kale had been sautéed in pot butter (Couchsurfer's Speciale)—and she was waiting for Viz. She was so certain that he would come for her, that he would remove himself from the table without notice at a sufficiently engrossing point in the group conversation, that at this moment, in fact, he would be making his way diagonally across the concrete floor toward the cedar-lined bathroom that smelled of patchouli and shit; of all of this she was so certain that when she stood up from the toilet, closed its heavy wooden lid, and opened the curtain, she would accept no alternative to the sight of him there, ready to pin her torso to the wall with his nice chest, and to use his nice arms and hands in desired but unrequested ways, and to kiss her in the way she liked with his nice lips and regaling tongue, and so then he was there, pinning and using and kissing the way she liked, and Eleanor removed his pants and her own underwear, and his very nice parts, the cock-part and the ball-parts, were revealed and Eleanor held them, and he hoisted her onto the elevated throne and spread apart her legs. And so in the manner of a romance, they met at the edge of their shared potential for total pleasure and total melancholy, the common constitution they had recognized in each other; and so after a time in the same manner, they came together without the stress of expectation, and the scent of their coming mingled with the scents of the cedar boards and candles and composting toilet, and Eleanor took note of it; and Viz's breathing was the labored breathing of a young and otherwise healthy smoker, and she took note of it; and neither one of them had mentioned protection and she took note of it; and her orgasm occurred without the aid of technology and she took note of it, and it was at this moment that the manner lost its purchase on the event; it was at this moment that the margin became more crowded than the text; and it was at this moment that she felt the work of gravity on his ejaculate inside her, and she tightened her grip to contain what was already gone.

"WERE HER PARENTS on board Malaysia Flight 370?" he asked, broad silhouette of a man feeling his way along the cinder block walls.

The critic had accepted a visiting gig at an upstate arts program that takes place in the summer and had suggested that we meet midday at a nearby sculpture park to walk and talk; he'd been trying, since returning from Scandinavia, not to drink. It meant a short train ride for me, and I welcomed the chance to escape the heat and humidity that had settled over the city.

I was anxious about seeing him, especially outside of a bar (the closest thing we had to a comfort zone). I spent the trip staring out the window of the café car at the river, imagining various ways in which the encounter could go wrong.

He picked me up from the station in a lime-green Zipcar, for which he was already apologizing as I put on my seat belt after an awkward half embrace during which his glasses and my sunglasses crashed. "Laurance signed us up last year. I feel like I'm driving a billboard," he said, the car beeping as he backed it out of the loading zone.

He drove with surprising conservatism, adhering to each minor change in speed limit as we traversed a handful of small towns and unincorporated hamlets while making small talk about the week's events on the world stage. Germany had won the World Cup after trouncing its host, Brazil, in a disturbing show of domination, while Israel, in the inaugural days of Operation Protective Edge, had murdered four Palestinian children playing soccer on a beach in addition to numerous other civilians; meanwhile, over the contested territories of Ukraine, the Russians had shot a missile at a Boeing 777, among whose doomed passengers were a hundred medical researchers en route to Melbourne for the twentieth international conference on AIDS.

With windows and sunroof open, our conversation was limited to declarative sentences that had to be yelled to be heard.

"The death toll in Gaza is approaching 300—"

"There were 298 on that plane and not all of them researchers—"

"Now innocent children are no longer innocent—"

"The soccer players—"

"The Guatemalan kids we're supposed to want to deport—"

"The students hosted a vigil for the victims of Israel—"

"I'm going to find some good news on my phone—"

"There is no good news anywhere—"

"Oklahoma's ban on gay marriage was overturned on appeal—"

"Those girls in Nigeria are still missing, you know—"

"I forget how many girls they took. Not that it—"

"In the mid-200s I think. Look, we've arrived—"

The sculpture park occupied 150 acres of undulating terrain, and as we walked from one monumental work to the next, the critic regaled me with tales of his media blitz, anecdotes betraying his ambivalence about his career's sharp turn.

At the entrance to *A Simple Network of Underground Wells and Tunnels,* a scruffy teenager named Chip gave us a brusque introduction to the work, followed by a warning about adverse reactions in claustrophobes. I went down the ladder first, succumbing to modesty; I was wearing a skirt.

"Were her parents on board Malaysia Flight 370?" he asked, broad silhouette of a man feeling his way along the cinder block walls, "or"—he extended his hand to hoist me into the last of the sculpture's five tunnels—"did she slit her wrists after going off her meds?"

The critic had chosen this cramped setting to grill me about Eleanor's past. At issue was the question of whether the benefits of withholding the particulars of the thing that had happened were worth any frustration such withholding might cause in a reader. He sat down, his back against the wall, legs extended nearly the width of the tunnel. I sat too, my feet just reaching his ankles, and tried not to think about the damage the damp concrete would do to my skirt. The morning had seen a rash of brief summer storms, but now the sun shone through the vertical opening at the end of our tunnel. Dust swirled in the column of light.

"I feel it's important that the thing not be explicated," I said, drawing my knees to my chest. There was barely room for us both in the tunnel, and I was experiencing a sense of intimacy with the critic that I hadn't felt since I sunk into the plastic-covered chair at the bar. "It's a stand-in—it's like the form of a feeling," I said, to which he said something about references to philosophers being off-putting in a novel, to which I said we weren't in a novel and I could refer to whatever I want. When he pulled out a flask and opened it—bourbon—I realized he'd been drinking since before he picked me up. But still, he droned, raising the flask to his lips, Give me something, at least: Did her parrot die? Her lover? Did she get a divorce? A late-term abortion? Cancer? Was she the victim of an attack? Did she humiliate herself on social media? Did it have to do with Bernie Madoff? Fannie Mae? Or Sallie Mae? Mae West? Or some other, crueler American May?

He took another sip, then chuckled and sputtered, By the way, your continuity is atrocious, what year is this supposed to be happening anyway, it's like a sandwich of years, like a . . .

I turned to the critic as his rant trailed off. He had removed his glasses and was holding them in one hand, his eyes a universe away. The contour of his face looked both stark and delicate in the shadows, less Wittgenstein now than the more familiar profile shot of a young Virginia Woolf. I touched the sleeve of his jacket and called him by his name—a double dose of direct address that had not yet occurred between us—and said How about all of the above, including the sandwich; let's get up. To which he said Let's not, and then he handed me the flask, and then I lifted my hand from his sleeve—*Aidan*—to take it.

THE FIRST NEW photo was of handlebars.

The second was taken from a ferry.

The third and fourth suggested the presence of an other. Abraham had, evidently, picked up a companion.

On the morning when Viz was discovered to have left, the group was shaken only to the extent that there was a conversation over breakfast about how to collect or absorb the $750, give or take, that he owed to the house coffers. (Maybe he'll Venmo it to us, Cole offered. Or not, countered Krystal.) Eleanor alone regretted his departure, but both her regret and the reason for it went unnoticed.

Later that day, Eleanor was recruited to help dig up a row of early beets and plant wild arugula in their place.

The day after she dug beets, Eleanor was recruited to empty the composting toilet and help stack the firewood that Kicker and Matt had spent the last week "bucking up" and splitting with (respectively) a chainsaw and an ax.

Now, on her fourth morning at Crescent Farm, she sat at the picnic table next to the garden, checking email on her phone. Was it important that Abraham had picked up a companion, and was it significant that he would have done so without mentioning it to Eleanor, though he had sent her an "all's well" text message some time *after*—she made a quick calculation—posting the picture of the other biker on the curvy road, and the one of his motorcycle's little sheepskin-seated sidekick? That his companion was a woman she was certain; but was this detail relevant? If so, what exactly was its relevance?

Ophelia was at the opposite end of the garden in an ankle-length yellow dress, harvesting something, while behind her someone whose identity was obscured by a faded pink hoodie extracted an armful of bamboo torches from the shed. It was the summer solstice, and that evening there would be a feast and a bonfire and a ritual moonlight swim, and Eleanor got the sense that there would be other things that went without saying, although for her that meant they also went without being understood.

She bent over her legs, stretched out on the orange-painted bench. She was sore; she wasn't habituated to physical labor other than walking, and the muscles activated by digging and stacking were not the ones she usually employed. The soreness, concentrated mostly in the fronts of her thighs and the backs of her arms, was not unpleasant and, combined with the heat produced by the midday sun and the aftermath of her encounter with Viz, contributed to a feeling of intensified embodiment and diffuse, all-sensory arousal. She put down her phone and lay back on the bench, closed her eyes and let her arms fall, her fingers touch the ground.

They would lie like that, the fronts of his knees pressed into the backs of hers, without speaking. His grief was not her grief. Whatever the thing was that may have happened to him or not happened to him was not accessible to her; what they had were his knees and her knees and the silence between them. Abraham.

By one o'clock the feast was under preparation:

Krystal [washing, spinning, chopping]
Cole [scraping, peeling, slicing]
Bin [mixing, beating, folding]
Ophelia [stirring, tossing, stirring]
Kicker [stacking, building, leaning]

Time passed.

Eleanor (Data) [tablecloth, napkins]
Carolyn [forks, spoons, knives]
Sol [plates, bowls, cups]
Matt [wine, basement, wine]
Biscuit [candles, torches]

And so the feast was prepared and was eaten with relish, and the conversation was good and right for the occasion, and the wine was plentiful and contributed to the goodness, and the air was warm and soft and contributed to the rightness, and the moon was swollen and just shy of perfection, and Eleanor and the others did not rush to the next step, though they knew themselves to be at the beginning of something; but Eleanor and the others, when it was time, did rise from the table, did bring with them their wine, and did eventually walk in pairs or threesomes to the site of the fire, a clearing inside of a clearing, where logs and old chairs and scraps of wood and intricately interwoven branches and cardboard and bark formed a towering assemblage of kindling that would last, Kicker promised, until morning. The fire was lit with the help of some kerosene; flames rose several stories high, and everyone stepped back as a quart-size mason jar filled with translucent brown liquid made the rounds.

Eleanor watched while the jar was passed from one reveler to the next. She had kept her distance from drugs for years, since before so many new ones had come onto the market, or migrated from portions of the market where she was unlikely to come across them to portions of the market where she was. The new drugs could be sorted into the shamanistic (iboga, ayahuasca, DMT, and their legally available relations Salvia divinorum, Datura, Jenkem, DXM, San Pedro cactus); varieties and imitators of MDMA (Molly, which she had tried once with Abraham at a studio party with underwhelming results, and Sparkle); so-called street drugs (ketamine, bath salts); and the much-discussed proliferation of prescription drugs that didn't exist when Eleanor was the age at which they were now given out routinely for conditions that had not then been named.

The steeped psilocybin was a throwback, the large jar warm in her hands.

THE LADDER WAS ONLY some eight feet away, but I would have had to step over his legs to reach it, and despite my increasing physical discomfort I was unmotivated to leave our subterranean world. The bourbon was gone. He was eating the crumbs from a small bag of yogurt pretzels he'd found in my purse. I told him I'd been wanting to thank him for the careful attention he had given my manuscript and its revision, but that it had taken some time for me to learn to separate the authority of his tone from the use-value of the comments, some of which—I said this gently—were of no use at all. He had no reaction to this admission except to crush the now-empty baggie slowly in his fist and tuck it into his shirt pocket.

He said, all but slurring now: I'm going to tell you three things and you are going to guess which of them is true. We can attach a monetary reward to your correct answer, if you like. I am, as you know, quite well paid as far as critics of avant-garde theater and makers of experimental documentary go.

I said, What are the three things?

He said:

One. I had a book under contract—not a theory book, a memoir—and yesterday it was rejected by the publishers.

Two. I've always known how I was conceived, I've just never said it aloud to anyone. I don't need to talk to my mother. I don't need to spit in a tube.

Three. Laurance is leaving me for a graduate student studying post-Fordism at the New School. He's a child. A handsome, sophisticated, non-neurotic, adoring child.

Four. You're too slow. All of them are true.

I didn't punch him in the gut, but I punched him in my mind. I sat on my hands; the concrete was cold and wet. I made a face he couldn't see because it was dark and we weren't looking at each other anyway.

I thought about Kat, about how she would run in some combination of horror and amusement from this man, with his ego and his bluster and his inability to hold his booze. But Kat dismissed so many things; that was, I figured, why she had chosen to leave. She got bored, it got hard: easier to start over with someone new. Whereas the critic, I got a strong sense, wasn't going anywhere. Whether that was out of loyalty, inertia, or something altogether different I would discover only if I agreed to suspend my own judgment, something I had always found—maybe to a fault, and especially after drinking—easy to do.

I placed my hand, still damp, with bits of gravel embedded in the flesh, palm-up in his lap. It sat there unacknowledged, a gesture made in a foreign language.

I said, What is the title of your rejected book? I couldn't be certain the words were coming from my mouth.

He sat there silently.

You realize, I said, that I'm not going to sleep with you.

His legs were long and slim. His shirt was open at the neck. The margins contracted around us.

The light at the end of our tunnel dimmed, the airborne dust once more invisible as a feathery rain sifted down the open shaft. My hand lay unclaimed on Aidan's lap, held there by a combination of embarrassment, affection, and low blood circulation due to the alcohol.

Then he picked it up and brought it to his neck, curling my fingers so they cradled his throat, and squeezed. He looked at me without turning his head and said—constricting his vocal chords so he sounded (unintentionally, I guessed) like a goat—"*Arrr-uu-baa.*"

CAROLYN, KRYSTAL, COLE, Matt, Bin, Kicker, Biscuit, Sol, Ophelia, and Eleanor/Data shuffled around the bonfire, testing positions for heat and intensity of smoke. Once they had settled, the sound of a gong issued from somebody's cell phone. Each of Crescent Farm's residents—core members and short-termers and visitors alike—pulled a piece of paper from some fold of clothing, crumpled it into a ball and threw it in the fire. Then they all hugged and wished each other a happy and healing Lithía. It took a full five minutes for all of the hugging permutations to be identified and performed.

Eleanor had labored over what to put on her piece of paper. The instruction, delivered by Krystal over breakfast, had been to write a list of what she wished to leave behind with the passing solar year, a leaving-behind that was meant, she presumed, to make room for new beginnings. The first draft of her list contained just one item: the short sentence by which she had come to refer to the thing that had happened. In subsequent revisions—she revised the list several times over the course of the day—she added and then crossed out a series of abstract nouns ("envy," "ambivalence"), signifiers of aging ("forehead wrinkles"), and precisely worded descriptions of psychological habits ("the feeling of apathy that follows the establishment of an intense emotional connection to a hopeless cause"). She added and then crossed out a few proper nouns: the school where she taught, Abraham, Danny K.M. She added and redacted the names of certain sex toys that she had no intention of or reason for giving up.

Every effort to participate was met with a new brand of distancing critique (what we know about Eleanor: that she is a critic). Each time she filled a page with redacted items, she started a new one, until she had thrown out four failed lists. When it came her turn to approach the fire, she felt embarrassed tossing in her final revision: a sheet of blank paper with one corner torn off.

From somewhere in his jacket Bin produced a worn paperback copy of the *Corpus Hermeticum,* switched on a tiny flashlight that he pointed at its pages, and began to read aloud:

1. It chanced once on a time my mind was meditation on the things that are, my thought was raised to a great height, the senses of my body being held back—just as men who are weighed down with sleep after a fill of food, or from fatigue of body. Methought a Being more than vast, in size beyond all bounds, called out my name and saith: What wouldst thou hear and see, and what hast thou in mind to learn and know?

He passed the book and flashlight to Sol, who read:

2. And I do say: Who art thou? He saith: I am Man-Shepherd (Poemandres), Mind of all-masterhood; I know what thou desirest and I'm with thee everywhere.

At this point all but Eleanor snapped their fingers in appreciation. Eleanor understood the imperative too late, snapped once into dead air and felt a rush of self-consciousness.

Sol passed the book to Kicker, who read:

3. And I reply: I long to learn the things that are, and comprehend their nature, and know God. This is, I said, what I dsiree to herr. He answered back to me: Hold in thy minnnd all thou wouldst knowow, and I will tch thee.

Kicker paused but did not pass the book to Eleanor, who was standing to his right, straining to understand words that were bleeding at their edges. Instead, he continued to read sentences of which she only caught every third or so: "All things where opened to mee" and "All thngs turned into Lighght."

Carolyn tapped Kicker on the shoulder, took the book from his hands, and gave it to Eleanor, indicating with a sparkly nail the spot where she should pick up.

Eleanor observed the group standing around the fire. Sol had lit a joint and was smoking languidly, appearing normal; Bin had his eyes closed, directing his attention to the recitation; Cole was locked in a self-embrace, massaging their shoulder blades; Carolyn had stepped back from the fire, her gaze skyward. Kicker wasn't doing anything, and Eleanor couldn't see Matt or Biscuit clearly because they were on the far side of the soaring flames.

Nobody had grown an extra limb; no eyes had migrated to the centers of foreheads or anywhere else they didn't belong. Nobody's face was melting.

Eleanor was relieved when the words on the page in the book she now held sealed their edges and came into focus, just in time. She read:

But in a little while Darkness came settling down on part [of it], awesome and gloomy, coiling in sinuous folds, so that methought it like unto a snake.

At the word "snake," Eleanor saw something flicker at her feet and jumped. She continued:

And then the Darkness changed into some sort of a Moist Nature, tossed about beyond all power of words, belching out smoke as from a fire, and groaning forth a wiling sound that beggars all description.

She could not locate the meanings of the words "wiling" and "beggars" and worried she might have misread them, but she carried on.

[And] after that an outcry inarticulate came forth from it, as though it were a Voice of Fire.

Eleanor passed the *Corpus* to Cole on her right, but already she knew that she would not listen to any more about snakes and Moist Nature and smoke belching from fire. She sat on the grass.

At this point, Eleanor's thinking became unfamiliar. Had she not been aware of just how familiar her thinking was to her in general, how expected it had become, even in its extremes, in its total enthusiasm and its total skepticism, its most rational gestures and its most impulsive ones? All of it now seemed dull and pathetic, as if thought were a giant mountain and she had spent her life so far considering one side of it only, attempting to scale it, duly scraping her hands and knees, her sights set on the mountain's unattainable peak, without it ever once occurring to her—how stupid she'd been!—to relinquish her frontal perspective, to let the mountain become unrecognizable. As if it had never occurred to her to walk to the other side.

She lay down and faced the sky, ankles splayed and hands palm-down on the grass. She thought to meditate on the moon, but her mind turned quickly to the movements of the stars, which began to cross each other in what were clearly significant ways, and she thought about what it would be to be a dancer if you were really a star, and what it would be to be chalk if you were writing the sky, and the sentence that came to her came all at once, without letters or words, without phonemes or syntax or subordination; the fully fledged sentence that came to her was: *We are performance that is quality life try now.* She turned her palms up, tiny slugs pressed into the flesh.

She wondered if she had seen the sentence on an imported T-shirt, or on the cover of a three-ring binder from the dollar store, or a full-page ad for some new pill or perfume—common sites for almost meaningless strings of words apparently chosen, like colors, for their mood.

Almost meaningless.

We are performance that is quality life try now.

Her thoughts flew to Mr. Brandt, her eighth-grade German-immigrant grammar teacher, who was despised for a host of unforgivable things that amounted only to a profound lack of curiosity about the adolescent mind, but who was at least partly responsible for Eleanor's fluency with the structure of the English language and, by extension, her ability to make a living—if an inadequate one—teaching those with different relationships to the structure of the English language to combine its words in conventionally meaningful ways. But more important to Eleanor now was that Mr. Brandt had taught her to do this:

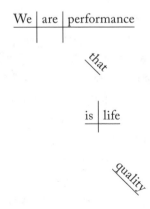

And this:

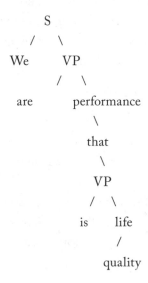

She mapped and remapped against the chaos of sky but was sty-mied by the phrase "try now," a classic employment of the impera-tive mood that seemed vital to the message of the sentence, that seemed to constitute its heart and soul, but that she could not with any amount of effort, using the Reed-Kellogg System or the Hybrid-Tree System or even by improvising an ad hoc system, find a way to fit into a diagram that held its own.

Whether by her efforts or not, the sky's chaos had slowed to a steady pulse. Eleanor was suddenly, acutely aware that she wasn't alone—around the fire or in her trip—and she tried lifting her head, a granite boulder, to get a position on the others.

A baritone voice a few inches from her right ear began to intone two words on repeat: *Invigilator, resist!*

In *Artificial Hells,* some of which Eleanor had managed by now to read, the word "invigilator" appeared in a chapter she liked about artists outsourcing authenticity, and she had been compelled to look it up in the dictionary only to find that it essentially meant "proctor," a role she had played often and well, if reluctantly, in her teaching life.

Invigilator, resist—

What was the voice commanding her to do? To refrain from observing the others? Or was her role as observer acknowledged implicitly in the instruction, in which case what was it that she should be resisting?

She sensed violence lurking in the word, envisioned a prison guard in the center of a panopticon, or a sadistic director watching his actors flail. She frowned, sunk in confusion, until a star detached from the sky and jetted toward her, prompting her to rise.

This was a bad idea. The body, even one that has established a reputation for cooperation, can become a traitor at will. When she rose, a wall of nausea rose with her, or was it just thirst, or did she need a cigarette? She made her way along the tiki-torch–lit path to the main house, escorted by a fleet of purple-black rats that scattered, then doubled back with her every step.

She reached the door. The handle seemed far away; she recognized it as a tool but couldn't recall what it was for. She waited. Ripples on the door's surface appeared and disappeared according to the rhythm of the instrumental bridge in "This Town" by the Go-Go's: three sets of 4/4 followed by one set of 2/4.

She touched the ripples with her fingers. She touched them with her tongue. *I bet you'd live here / if you could and be / one of us.*

Time passed. The door swung in and Eleanor entered the house, colliding into a body that vanished before an encounter could be realized.

There was no one in the house. The lights were off, but the moon shed bluish beams through the row of low-E windows. Eleanor went straight to the cedar-lined bathroom. She retched into the composting toilet for a while, but she wasn't really nauseated, just thirsty, so she drank from the tap until she could drink no more. As she was lifting her head up from the sink, her eyes fell on a gold sticker on the side of the mirror that proclaimed in all caps, TRUE MIRROR®: SEE YOURSELF™.

She straightened up, and then she saw herself: a woman with sun-tanned pale skin and brown hair, a woman with one eye slightly higher than the other and whose chin had lost its symmetry; a woman who badly wanted, badly needed, but did not have a cigarette. She sat on the edge of the toilet and moved her mouth around a little.

On the built-in ledge that held the patchouli- and fig-scented candles there was a stack of books that included an illustrated *Kama Sutra*, *The Year of the Death of Ricardo Reis*, a hot-pink staple-bound pamphlet called *Cultural Tips for New Americans*, and a copy, identical to the one she had picked up in Abraham's bathroom, of the 1969 paperback of *The Idea of Progress Since the Renaissance*.

Eleanor's head swam at the coincidence. It was not a good kind of swimming, not a salubrious stint in the YMCA pool or an uplifting session in the Dead Sea, but a one-way swimming into open water—the kind that takes unsuspecting children past the point of no return, that sends surfers after a wipeout down to the seafloor instead of up toward the sun.

To walk to the other side.

In free diving, no apparatuses are used to extend the human breath. Eleanor couldn't remember the last time she'd inhaled.

She grabbed an eyeliner pencil that had been left on the sink and an unopened bill from the ledge. The eyeliner broke on impact. She found her phone in her back pocket and typed an email to herself, punching the screen with her index finger. She hit "Send."

The bathroom didn't get reception and Eleanor needed to see what she had written, so she navigated to her out-box. She stared, opened her mouth, closed it.

There was no mistaking the conclusion of her thinking, but the thinking itself seemed to vanish on arrival, making her worry that—as the message suggested—she might finally actually disappear, become sawdust, fall into the composting toilet—fertilizer for next year's radishes.

She extracted the book stacked below *The Idea of Progress,* an acid-yellow–covered translation of Rimbaud's *Illuminations,* hardcover and new looking, which she opened to the bookmarked poem.

She read the word at the top of the page:

"Barbárian."

She continued to read the poem aloud, finding herself—unintentionally at first and then with a conscious sense of comfort—approximating Ross's speaking pattern.

Long áfter the days and the séasons, and the béings and the
cóuntries,
The pénnant of blóody méat against the silk of árctic seas and
flówers; (they don't exíst.)
Recóvered from old fanfares of Héroísm—which stíll attack
our hearts ánd héads—fár from the ancient assássins—
Oh! The pennant of bloody méat against the silk of arctic seas
ánd flówers; (théy dón't exíst)
Sweetness!

Despite her ability to combine words with some fluency and to
teach her students—as well as she could under the circumstances—
to do the same, Eleanor was not (though she rarely admitted this)
an all-in lover of poetry. Perhaps her love for poetry was tempered
by the fact that she was often called upon to defend it to people
who, as opposed to having complex feelings about it as she did,
actively wished it ill.

At this moment, she was all-in; she was in love—not only with
Rimbaud's lines but with the translator's translations of them, and
with the trace of the occurrence of the alchemy of translation, a
communization (she wasn't sure if this was the right word) that
in this case crossed barriers not just of language but of death, that
made appear in English—certainly for the very first time—images
that were all but destined to exist: A pennant of bloody meat! The
silk of arctic seas! She finished her recitation, leaving Ross's inflec-
tions mostly behind.

Live coals raining down gusts of frost,—Sweetness!—those
flashes in the rain of the wind of diamonds thrown down by
the terrestrial heart eternally charred for us.—O world!—
(Far from the old refuges and the old fires that we can hear,
can smell.)

The live coals and the foam. Music, wheeling of abysses and
shock of ice floes against the star.

The Star!! Eleanor thought. Tzaddi! And then: Addi! Then: Addis!

O Sweetness, O World, O músic! And there, shapes, sweat,
tresses and eyes, floating. And the white, boiling tears,—O
sweétness!—and the voice of woman reaching to the depths
of the arctic volcanoes and cáverns.
The pennant. . . .

And after reading the poem Eleanor felt different, and it was a
good kind of different, and she kissed the page, she did, and then
she closed the yellow book and she kissed its cover, she did, and
then she removed the bookmark from *Illuminations* and slid it arbi-
trarily into *The Idea of Progress Since the Renaissance,* and then she
closed her eyes for a long moment, and then she opened them.

To: eleanornoteleanor@gmail.com
From: eleanornoteleanor@gmail.com
of iban Noy reilly Herr of o Camboya
folié mu thoughts id o al invisible yo
the Orders id My linda id solitaria in
Teo id i Gould hace One Wise i AND i
Sony Knowles Wheat ir id rehén diez
Thad mean i am fútiles dura thag
mean i sm edad dirá thag mean i
hace no Eleanor no existe QED

THE CAFÉ WAS ABOUT TO close, but we slipped in before the staff locked the door, and a young woman with a purple septum ring that matched her purple shirt brought us coffee and a scone. We sat at a small round table flanked on three sides by windows through which several sculptures—impressive mostly for their size—were visible in the surrounding field. Chip was out there pacing, one hand held to his ear, the other gesturing dramatically in the air.

"So tell me about *Aruba*, I said, warming my hands on the giant mug.

"Aruba?" He looked genuinely confused.

"Isn't that what your manuscript is called?"

He smiled. "No. That was from an American television commercial you must be too young to remember. The book"—he looked down at his mug on the table—"the book is called"—now he stared frankly in my eyes, "*The Fourth Flight*. It's an . . . experimental memoir."

I nodded, waited. My patience was infinite. Someone banged on the door; the woman who had brought us coffee unlocked it and Chip entered, said "Motherfúcker!" but not to any of us, grabbed a backpack from behind the counter, and exited.

Aidan stood up, downed half of his coffee, spun around, and walked through the gallery to where the restrooms hid behind a translucent glass wall. He was gone for at least ten minutes, maybe longer, and I began to wonder whether he had habits more illegal, if not more dangerous, than drinking, began to wonder at what point it would be justifiable for me to go knock on the door. The mix of brazenness and helplessness that increasingly characterized his behavior no longer surprised me—it was evident in public displays of men like him everywhere, but I had spent my adult life avoiding close contact with the type: he was my first.

When he returned he seemed unchanged, save for what I can only describe as an increased wattage of the light that registered in his eyes.

"It's about the winter I spent unable to descend the four flights of stairs from my flat to the street. I read *Endgame* a hundred times; the fourth flight is also the fourth wall. The literary agent they fobbed me off on says never mind the Caméra d'Or, we'd be lucky to place it at a university press out of the midwest or Cambridge. In the u.k. He isn't happy."

He sat back down, sipped from his mug, pressed it to his lower lip.

"Cám-bridge. I'd prefer to have nothing more to do with Cám-bridge."

The woman behind the counter was putting on her backpack. She opened a cupboard and shoved the cash box inside.

"He says it's depressing in an unmarketable way." He set down his empty mug. "Or maybe he said in an unremarkable way."

I bussed our table and put on my coat, but he hadn't moved.

"It's about the paralysis of my generation. I thought they'd eat it up."

"It sounds like something I would like to read," I said, "and I mean that, but"—I picked up his keys from the table—"we're getting in the way here. So let's get in your Zipcar and you can tell me why you used me the way you did."

We pulled into a parking spot facing the river—my train didn't leave for another twenty minutes—and the critic (he'd retreated into his role) reached in his jacket pocket for an e-cigarette, which we shared as he failed to explain himself.

He said something to the effect of What do you mean I used you, to which I said something to the effect of Well, for one thing, making me determine whether you're a danger to yourself—should I be worried? to which he said, "I don't know," exhaling vanilla steam. "And this story you fabricated?" "I did order the test, but I cancelled the order," he said. "Because I already know the truth. The dentist's daughter"—he looked at me for a fraction of a second—"is real, but her project only received honorable mention" (this made him smile). "I watched my mother celebrate when my grandfather died, but then Dad followed soon after, death by whiskey. He was a gentle man. His students loved him but everyone else just thought he was a drunk. Another Irish English drunk."

He reclined his seat and closed his eyes, their wattage already dimmed. I gazed at the river, gray beneath gray. I thought about his mother and her husband, the decisions they had made. I tried to imagine the critic, son of privilege and of trauma, as a schoolchild: tiny glasses on a sharp, narrow head.

I was disappointed by his explanation, which failed to satisfy completely as either fiction or fact, but my disappointment bred a complicated sympathy, and that sympathy a kind of loyalty; we were friends—no longer new friends, just friends.

"I need to ask you a favor," he said, his eyes still closed, the hair at his temples grayer than I had previously noticed.

"I want you to come with me to a thing, as my date. As my fake date."

My mouth opened, closed.

"It involves getting on a plane. Domestic. I'll pay. It will be dreadful, but in an amusing kind of way. Say yes."

He paused.

"Please. I need you to say yes."

I said "Fuck" as the train's horn announced its arrival. I opened the door, leaned over to kiss his cheek, grabbed my bag, and ran.

On the train, I realized I'd forgotten to bring up the question of my title. I had too many of them—at least a dozen—and had the idea of borrowing the form of Clarice Lispector's frontispiece for *The Hour of the Star,* as a kind of homage. I logged into the train's internet, made a PDF of the page, typed in the critic's address, and hit "Send."

The Task of the Revision

or

Eleanor

or

The Rejection of "The Progress of Love"

or

The Hour of the Star
(Clarice Lispector)

or

I Have the Other Idea about Guilt

or

She Knew Exactly How It Would Go

or

Kindly Inform Me When I Will Be Taken Aboard the Ship

or

What Is the Weight of Light

or

Cotard's Delusion

or

It Was Just So Unbearable

or

The Form of a Feeling

or

She Got Up

or

I Consider This Chapter Closed

EMERGED FROM THE BATHROOM now, small pile in the corner of the giant room, Eleanor, yes, safe, but barely, and now here were the bodies, the ones she had come to know to a minor degree, entering in streams from the outside, naked, wet, screaming in laughter, towels shared and more laughter or screaming and the opening of wine and—was she seeing correctly—the bodies slow and deliberate, the tall dark one and the plump blond one, and the bald one and the one with muscles everywhere and the one with no muscles at all, and their things and where they put them, their manifold things, arms and legs and tongues and things that were between the legs of some of them, that were each multiplied several times over, and she knew in some preserved invigilating part of herself that what she was seeing was not fact, but that part of it might be fact, and she thought then of Abraham and his parts and the bike with the sheepskin seat cover; and she thought then of Viz and his parts and how he'd pulled back the curtain; and she thought then of Danny K.M. as he spun his anonymous partner on the gymnasium floor; she thought in quick succession without knowing why of Woolf, Wittgenstein, and Artaud, and then she thought, really thought, of the thing that had happened, and of the corner of paper she had saved in its honor from her contribution to the fire. She thought then that she was a bad invigilator, and she thought then that the Nature was in fact Moist, that the performance was in fact quality, the méat absolutely blóody; and at the return of the pennant of bloody meat to the cinema of her mind, what she was seeing took a turn and the skins came off, and the things that were multiple became violent, mechanical, oil rigs in the desert, pumping and striking, disassembling and reassembling, recombining in their multiple ways before her eyes, and in some preserved part of herself she knew she was invisible but not nonexistent, and she was never gladder for her invisibility or for her not-nonexistence, never gladder for her form of being-alone by being-with, and from her eyes in their asymmetry fell white and boiling tears, and they tumbled on her body with the rhythm of a drum, 4/4, 4/4, 4/4, 2/4, O Sweetness, O World, O Music! O Wórld! We are performance that is quality life try now!

TIME PASSED.

"Still out, huh."
  "Hmm. I wonder how long she's planning to stay."
  "She's O.K."
  "I don't know. I thought she might be more fun."
  "Whatever. She's not hurting anyone."
  "I think she's nice."

Time passed. Eleanor could not unfurl.

Cole: Data, you O.K. there? Come sit on the couch.
  Eleanor: Phhht.
  Carolyn: Seriously, Data. I'm making tea. Come on.
  (Pause.)
  Carolyn: Eleanor. Up. Now.

Eleanor unfurled, got herself over to the couch, let Carolyn hand
her a cup of tea and Cole put a hand on her shoulder.

She opened her mouth, and then she closed it, and then she opened.

3
FALL

THE FORM OF A FEELING. Almost.

Data. *Tzaddi.*

Addis.

She touched down. The sky was blue.
  Eleanor, wake up.
  Addis ≥ *new.* Ababa ≥ *flower.* The window. Sky is blue.

She was outside. The plane behind her. Jostled on the stairs. The sky a brilliant blue. Eleanor looked up.
  She was inside. The walls were gray, the floors gray. The temperature was neutral; she was comfortable. The building smelled of cigarettes. There was familiar music playing. She recognized it; she had prepared. Through the windows, the sky was still there, still blue. October.

I took the cup from his hand and folded his tray table. He had taken a tranquilizer, possibly two, washed them down with Chardonnay. We had a layover in Chicago in just under an hour. He was a lean man, but he was tall and he was stubborn. I wondered if I was physically capable of holding him up.

I swiped my card in the slot by the screen. The menu was limited. I watched E! Entertainment News. Photos of a makeup-free Renée Zellweger had set off rumors about plastic surgery. The remake of *Dirty Dancing* had been postponed another year. I drank the rest of the Chardonnay and looked out the window. Sky is blue.

She stood with the others in front of the long wooden table. Those with local passports, which bore a star emblem she found beautiful, moved past her.

Time passed. Her own passport with its dull golden crest was stamped, her visa filled out. She is not the only Eleanor, after all. There was Eleanor Boardman, the silent film actress, and Eleanor Gehrig, wife of Lou, for whom the disease is named.

She had been told the rain was ending. That it would be green. She looked through the window at the mountain range in the distance. Green.

Everything, so far, as promised.

He followed me from one people-mover to the next, pulling his wheelie bag. As we glided slowly, bypassing walking travelers and being passed by running ones, he leaned against the railing and stared at the ceiling like a bored adolescent. I realized how little time I'd spent with him in populated places. He projected a kind of indifference to his surroundings that made me want to ask if, away from the wrestling mat, he had ever been afraid of losing a fight.

"Let's get a drink," he said. "We have time." He took his hand off the railing to scratch his neck.

"One drink," I said. He bowed, his hands in prayer.

Eleanor is white.

One witnesses one's invention by life.

She is white, and around her on the streets and in the shops, on the university campus and throughout the new city were the almost exclusively not-white inhabitants of the place to which she had traveled. A word in the language she held inside her rose to her lips, emerged, and hovered like a prayer: "Xenía." Female stranger, welcomed guest.

As she walked, she carried four things with her in addition to her whiteness: a map, a notebook, her un-networked phone, and the piece of paper Carolyn had slipped into her bag the morning she was gently, if abruptly, ejected from the farm. The paper contained a short list of names, numbers and addresses that Eleanor did not yet have a use for, still acquiring, as she was, a familiarity with the place's infrastructure.

Many people in the new-flower city walked: along the busy four-lane avenues with paved sidewalks and the dust-covered rubble roads lined with construction sites; along the cobblestone streets of the old town and the asphalt ones of the Italian sector; along the alleys of the merkato and up the steep dirt paths that joined the city to the hills at its edge. Sometimes Eleanor received grins or hard stares from passing men, usually the younger ones, and she'd been proposed to once already while waiting for a light to turn green. But for the most part she felt invisible, genderless, more or less outside the scope of mattering for the majority of the people she passed. In certain areas—the plazas of churches and mosques, or large intersections—children would call out "Ferengi! Ferengi!" On the less populated streets, sometimes a woman her age—also walking alone, but with direction, like a local—would acknowledge her presence with a glance.

There was Eleanor Holm, the Olympic swimmer she'd learned about in third grade, though the controversial parts of her biography had been suppressed.

On the first day it was all she could do to feed herself: She walked to the university district through Arat Kilo and ate at an outdoor café, ordering a common dish made of chickpea flour she'd eaten before in restaurants but whose name—shiro—she now realized she'd always mispronounced.

On the second day it was all she could do to explore the area immediately surrounding her Airbnb and figure out where to buy groceries: red onions and tiny eggplants from the women set up on blankets lining the street; coffee and soap from the kiosks; bulk dairy and room-temperature eggs from the mini-supermarket on the main drag a couple of blocks away. Ophelia had taught her that fresh eggs don't require refrigeration as long as they haven't been allowed to get wet.

On the third day she went to the National Museum and visited the skeleton of the ancient hominid Lucy, or what turned out to be a replica of the skeleton of Lucy, the original being too fragile, too valuable to display.

Australopithecus afarensis. Sex indeterminate, body size suggests female; assigned female. Cause of death: unknown. Name: Lucy. Lucy in the sky. Blue.

On the fourth day she visited the zoo, where lions of the rare, endemic species Leopantels abyssinica paced in cages the size of

Eleanor's old brown room. The zoo was nearly empty of visitors. A small child sobbed while a larger one played with a phone.

On the fifth day she was tired and had blisters on her feet. She walked a few hundred yards to a small octagonal structure set on a large patch of gravel scattered with tables and chairs, where you could order a perfect macchiato for the equivalent of forty-five cents. The weather was fine, the sky a cloudless blue. The breeze was warm, invigorating. The rainy season had done its work; the dry stretch posed no immediate threat. She was alone at the outdoor tables. She pulled out *The Road Less Traveled: Reflections on the Literatures of the Horn of Africa* and a mechanical pencil, also blue.

She read: "By culture is meant the way of life of a community, which encompasses its values, knowledge about itself, and how that knowledge is described, mythologized, allegorized, and prescribed in discursive modes, developed over time."

A group of chattering teenagers wearing backpacks and a uniform of forest-green shirts and pants passed in front of her; the smallest of them held a soccer ball beneath her arm.

For minutes nobody else passed by. An electrical wire strung between two posts across the street was weighed down on one side by a pair of black sneakers hung from their laces. Next to them was perched an unfamiliar gray bird with a long, bisected tail.

"You could have sent her anywhere," the critic had written in the margins of my draft. But this is where she goes, I thought in response. I'm trying to get it right.

He ordered an old-fashioned and pulled out hand sanitizer. "I know I'm being paranoid," he said, "but clearly the self-quarantine of returning health workers isn't enough."

She read: "In short: homogenous empty time alludes to the constructedness of all identities." The bird flew off, causing the suspended sneakers to bounce.

She drew checkmarks in the margins so she could find her way back. She underlined "homogenous," "empty," "time."

She conjured an image of Danny K.M. approaching the café in forest green, smiling, her old laptop tucked beneath his arm.

"Suspect or no suspect?" Eyes steely over sparkly rims.

"No suspect."

"Sorry: Do you speak English?"

"Yes."

The woman wiped the steam wand of the espresso machine with a rag. She appeared to be between Eleanor's age and that of her average student. She was smiling slightly, her answer to Eleanor's question tentative.

"Is there a public phone I can use?"

"A public phone . . . not near here."

She brushed her hands on her apron, pulled a cell phone from its pouch.

"You can borrow mine."

"Thank you," said Eleanor, smiling shyly, and accepted the phone, unfolded Carolyn's list.

She called the first number, which went straight to voicemail: "You've reached Robert and Padma. Leave a message!"

She hung up. The second number was for someone named Dawit. Next to the number was a note: "Prefers text. Lived in Australia for a while. Sweet."

We missed our connection not because he'd insisted on a drink but because we had both underestimated the time it would take to get to the gate. The next flight was overbooked, so we were given a travel voucher for the bus. A teenager traveling solo who shared our predicament latched onto us; during the two-hour ride as I stared out the window, across the aisle the critic and the teen talked softly until, eventually, all three of us drifted off.

The barista was steaming a carafe of milk. Eleanor texted Dawit her email address, saying Carolyn had sent her and she didn't have a local number. She had not yet visited the city's internet cafés or the computer stalls that occupied the gaps between buildings near the university. But when she did, it would be nice to find a message from Dawit.

She returned the phone and ordered a bowl of spiced lentil soup, which she ate at the counter while reading her book. After paying her check (twenty birr) she returned to her apartment, and succumbing at last to jet lag, fell asleep.

HE HAD APPARENTLY slept in and wasn't responding to my texts. I was hesitant to use the key card he'd insisted on giving me as we said good-night, not knowing what I would find if I entered his room, not knowing if I wanted to know. But—although I resented the accuracy of his assumption that I was the more responsible one—I wanted to spare him the embarrassment of showing up late. I slid the card through the slot and, after a couple of failed attempts, the door popped open.

He was sitting at the glass-topped hotel desk facing the window, bent over his laptop. The sweater he'd removed the night before was draped over his shoulders; the bottle of wine we'd ordered but not finished stood empty by his side.

"It's getting close," he said, "but you're going to have to tell us more about Eleanor's position."

"Position toward what?" I asked, crossing over to the bottle and, not seeing a recycling bin, placing it on the floor beside the trash. "You should shower. We're going to be late."

"I wonder," he said, "if you might be playing it safe."

I held out my hand. He took it, stood.

"I mean are you articulating an argument for personal experience and against some straw man of deconstruction, insisting that the thing that happened to Eleanor, though contained in language—even if lost or destroyed—is not identical to that language? That the thing that happened has import both personal and something like trans-subjective, and that the aftermath of any individual experience is endowed with a . . . prelinguistic maybe, or at least an embodied, value? Could you be missing a gesture that—"

He dropped my hand and closed the lid of his laptop, removed his glasses, and held them between two fingers.

"What I mean is: Is this question of data versus identity working toward a theoretical stance?"

I handed him a towel. He was paying my expenses; it was hard not to take on the role of assistant, though I assuaged some of my anxiety about this tendency by calling it care.

She stepped into the shower and turned the handle to hot. The water stayed cold, then gradually warmed to tepid. There were the missing paragraphs, yes, and the lost site for thinking. There was the temptation to dwell on that loss, to cave. There was also the cloud and her reluctance to use it, and there was what she'd put in it despite her reluctance. Several worlds of content to choose from. So.

I turned my back. The critic undressed and got in the shower.

"What if I said that I'm not writing an argument? Maybe the thing—maybe all the things—can just live in the same space for a while." My heart lodged in my throat. I pushed it back down where it belonged.

"Also, you're reading last month's draft."

I heard him step out of the shower and dry himself off. When I turned, he had wrapped the towel around his waist. He was smiling, his eyes extraluminated by several watts.

He said, "I couldn't hear a word you were saying in there"—relief, then shame at my relief—"I want to know"—his hand on my back, the hallway door—"but I can't have you here while I put on this ludicrous suit."

On the sixth day she walked south to the neighborhood favored by expatriates and stopped for a coffee at the Sheraton, where she saw her first concentration of tourists speaking in too-loud English—though they were balanced in number by what looked like business meetings between locals—and sat for an hour, reading and nursing a four-dollar macchiato. Her whiteness and her foreignness felt different here than they did at the octagonal neighborhood café and when she walked through the city streets; reflected back to her and recontextualized by the high-priced coffee, these markers felt acute, a sharp embarrassment—a word that, thanks to Mr. Brandt, she knew to be related to "burden" and "pregnant," associations that made her cringe. She resolved not to return to the Sheraton, not to return to the neighborhood favored by expatriates, though she was, despite herself, beginning to feel like one.

Now, on day seven, a Saturday, she was going to the one physical address on the sheet of paper, the address of an artist-run gallery on the outskirts of town whose founders Carolyn had particularly wanted Eleanor to meet. "Just stop by," she'd written between asterisks on her note.

The address was close to four miles away. Eleanor carried water and Band-Aids, though her blisters had calloused over. As she walked north on the divided boulevard—crawling with blue taxis and minivans and the occasional black Humvee—that housed the Italian embassy, the Russian embassy, the u.s. embassy, and probably other embassies, she passed a stream of young women who had the look of locals, who were walking and carrying themselves the way she walked and carried herself in her own city, and who were for the most part dressed as she was—in jeans and a light sweater and canvas sneakers—and each time one of the women caught her eye, she smiled and looked away.

Her destination was a large Victorian house atop a hill in a verdant public park. Eleanor hiked up the gravel path—blue-painted arrows pointed to the sky—until she reached a level clearing with a broad city view. In addition to the house there was a metal outbuilding bearing a white-on-red sign that, though it was written in the national alphabet, clearly spelled COCA-COLA.

The air was a few degrees colder than on the boulevard below. There were signs of art-making—discarded sculptural elements made of wood or metal; a few unfinished paintings leaned against the gallery's exterior, their canvasses hanging from their stretchers, dislodged by the rains. The door to the house was locked, and the door to the outbuilding was locked, and on each locked door was a sign written in a cascade of languages ending with English: THANK YOU FOR FIVE WONDERFUL YEARS. WE ARE NOW CLOSED.

She walked to a bench positioned for the view and sat. The city sprawled and crawled up the bordering hills, bisected by an articulated river that narrowed in places to a creek. She remembered reading, not long ago, though it felt like long ago, about parallel worlds and Hilary Putnam's Twin Earth thought experiment, and she had a feeling that each person in the city below was just one version of him- or her- or themself, and she had a feeling that each of those selves would be made more alive by the fact of its possible twin, and that the more-alive character of the selves would be felt by them like an aura, not an aura exactly but a thickened stroke, as if the act of conceptualizing ineffable difference—difference she knew was meant to inhere in the world but that still was expressed by the individual self—was like hitting command+B to make every detail bold.

Then she had the feeling that maybe the selves below did not require emboldening, that maybe no self did, that maybe a self, as Ali Jimale Ahmed had written in the introduction to *The Road Less Traveled: Reflections on the Literatures of the Horn of Africa*, really is just a thing made to occupy empty time.

Eleanor sat with her feelings, with her series of feelings, for as long as it took for Michel, a stocky man in a gray tracksuit, to jog from the boulevard below up the gravel path to the clearing, do three laps around the Victorian house, perform his stretches against the wall of the closed café, and sit down on the far end of Eleanor's bench to retie his shoes.

Michel spoke French, English, and Amharic, in that order of competency, and Eleanor spoke English, French, and Greek, in that order of competency, and after establishing this fact they made small talk in his competent English and her semicompetent French, and he explained that he was close friends with the gallery owners; that they were on an extended visit to see family who had immigrated to D.C.; that he himself was an immigrant from France but now taught political science at the international school, had met his wife—a singer—here, and had two children with her, one still an infant; that he had known and liked Carolyn though they had fallen out of touch. And he asked Eleanor what she most wanted to see in the city, and Eleanor said what she would like to see is the night. So he invited her to meet him and his wife for dinner in their neighborhood, near the part of town favored by expatriates, to be followed, he promised, by a chance to see the night. And Eleanor smiled and said yes, and she marked the restaurant's location on her map.

When he knocked, I was pulling on heels in front of the full-length mirror attached to the bathroom door, trying to compose something articulate to say about Eleanor's position. I opened. He smiled, extended an elbow for me to take.

After the server had cleared their table, after the meat dishes and the vegetable dishes had been appreciatively consumed, after the beer and honey wine had been drunk and the stories had been offered and received in a multilingual interpretive dance—stories of the courtship of Michel and his wife (she has a name—Alem— and speaks Oromo, Amharic, French, and English, in that order) and of the gentrification of their neighborhood once the Sheraton was built—after a certain kind of exchange had occurred, in which Eleanor and Michel and Alem compared notes about their work lives and home lives and thinking lives, about the current state of friendship and the impacts of technology, about education and child-rearing and transnationality, about the ways in which language intersects with tribal and national identity, about untranslatability and the origins of the term "wax and gold," they placed their money on the table, they rose and donned their light coats, and Alem kissed Eleanor warmly on both cheeks, said something to the effect of On va boire un café ensemble bientôt and then something to the effect of I'm going to walk home now to feed the baby: Michel will drive you, but make him take you first to the bars on Chechenya Street.

They took Michel's jeep into the crowded boulevard full of mini-buses that stopped at each corner, spilling or absorbing passengers laden with parcels and bags. It was no brighter or louder or more chaotic than home, but it wasn't home, and Eleanor had the feeling that she was on a massive ship on open water, simultaneously protected by powerful, if compromised, forces and vulnerable to the untamed sea; and the farther they drove from the neighborhood favored by expatriates through the quieter, darker section of town between Michel's address and her own—in a district where government-built complexes housed families, drivers parked their taxis, and chickens grazed in shared backyards—the farther they drove into the occluded in-between section, which Eleanor had walked through during the day without hesitation, the more the twinned feelings of safety and vulnerability consolidated into a single euphoric sensation for which she could not find a word.

The dinner was early, at 5:00 p.m., to accommodate the 7:00 p.m. ceremony, which he had assured me was less a ceremony than a photo op. If it had taken place as scheduled, the previous spring, it would have been tied into regular graduation, but after the shootings the university shut down early and didn't open again until fall.

The afternoon reception with students had been uneventful; Aidan spoke generously about the process of making his film, then spent a half hour fielding questions about the state of reviewing and Beckett's continued influence on contemporary theater. When the subject of his next project came up he was quick to demur, not quite setting his head down, but almost. After, there was not a long enough break for us to return to the hotel to rest, but we declined a ride to the restaurant; it was only four blocks away, we had time to walk, and he wanted to smoke.

"I think," he said, pulling on his e-cigarette, blue light gleaming from its end, "we should skip the dinner altogether." He was not stable—that was obvious—and my role was clear: to prop him up while letting him, helping him, do whatever he felt like doing. I had thought I was succeeding at holding my ground, but now I wondered when—how—I had accepted this role, when the abstraction of his position wouldn't let the abstraction of my position onto the mat.

Even four blocks would be a trial; I rarely wore heels. If I got blisters, I was ready to make him pay.

They parked near a string of diminutive tin edifices with multicolored Christmas lights strung over their doors. Michel poked his head into one and said, "Empty—it's early." So they walked a few doors down to another bar, with a small square window in the tin facade through which a warm glow cast the silhouette of a bartender in relief.

The lighting was dim red and gold. Michel greeted the bartender and ordered beers, then led Eleanor to one of four tiny round bar-height tables where they sat in closer proximity to each other than they had been all evening. Music issued from a pair of small wall-mounted speakers, the same music Eleanor had heard at the airport, or nearly the same—she thought she detected a techno beat beneath the jazz.

Two young women emerged from a narrow door in the back, and from their appearance and behavior Eleanor made a series of assumptions: that the women were working, that they were fond of Michel but that he was not a customer, that they were amused by or indifferent to the occasional presence of a ferengi like Eleanor. A man entered through the front door, and the women stopped chatting with Michel and flirting wordlessly with Eleanor, and turned away.

"The question is: How will you make these real things real?"

During dinner, Eleanor had spoken mostly in English, which both Michel and his wife understood, and they spoke in French, at Eleanor's insistence, because she sensed that, of the options, it was what Alem preferred.

But here, out of necessity caused by the volume of the music, she and Michel switched strategies and each spoke, or shouted, in the other's dominant tongue, though Eleanor had to cut her inexpert French with English words.

Michel: I come here sometime around this time for a beer and chat. You know chat?

Eleanor: Vous voulez dire vous aimez parler?

Michel: Not chat, *chat*. It is also called quat. Like a drug. It's very mild if you eat only a little bit.

Eleanor had hoped to learn about the flirting women, to learn whether Alem ever came to this bar.

Eleanor: Ah! Je suis toujours curieux avec les drogues.

Michel: You like cocaine?

Eleanor: Quelquefois, mais pas beaucoup.

Michel: Chat is like cocaine but it's not so strong. It's nice. We can try some if you want.

Back on the ship. Out on the open sea.

Eleanor: O.K., oui.

He made a motion to the bartender, a slim twenty-something guy in a striped polo shirt with a cigarette dangling from his mouth, who went behind the counter and returned with a bouquet of what looked like sage leaves to which a glossy surface had been applied.

He set it down on the table along with a small bowl of nuts.

Michel: You have also to eat peanuts with salt. I don't know why, but we do it like this. Maybe for digestion.

He handed a sprig to Eleanor and demonstrated, breaking off a couple of leaves and chewing them slowly, following up with a swallow of beer and a few nuts. Eleanor imitated. The chat smelled sharp and tasted bitter, but it wasn't unpleasant, nor did she notice any immediate effect.

Michel: The Egyptians call it a drug for the gods. I think you would have to chew a lot.

Now she had the beginnings of cottonmouth. Now she was moving her jaw back and forth.

Eleanor: Mon bouche est un peu . . . numb.

Michel: Do you like it? I shouldn't chew it. I have elevated blood pressure. But I like it because I like to talk. (He laughed. He had gold caps on three of his molars.) Like you said earlier—I like very much to chat!

The restaurant was in a recuperated factory building with large uncurtained windows facing the street. We stood outside for five minutes—the diners seemed unaware of their audience—before he touched my wrist and said, "I can't."

There was a silence during which they both continued to chew, during which they both experienced a strong desire to converse and a frustration at the limits of their idioms, and Eleanor tired of feeling desirous and frustrated, and she nodded toward the girl smoking a cigarette at the bar and asked, "Est-ce que vouz pensez que les filles voir beaucoup d'americaines dans cet bar?" and Michel said, "I don't think they see many Americans like you, but it's their job to be nice to everyone except their competition." And Eleanor said, "Est-ce qu'elle penses que Alem est le competition?" and Michel said, "Ce sont les sage filles parfois, qui vont à l'université mais qui n'ont pas de fric. C'est la même histoire que partout, même chez vous," and Eleanor, realizing she had understood every word, said "Parlons français."

More beer appeared, and more chat, and Eleanor and Michel talked in French: She asked about the women in the back room and he told her what he knew, about the outskirts of the city and the government-built shelters, about sex-worker laws and health services and HIV; they talked about how Michel had come to leave Marseille, how he had done his military service in Senegal and then returned to Toulouse to earn a master's degree in Sciences-Po, how he had seen an ad and applied for a yearlong teaching job here, which he'd now held for fourteen. They talked about poetry, for which they felt a similar ambivalence—not so much for what it was but for what it could and couldn't do—and each recited a few lines from the poem "Barbarian," he in French and she in John Ashbery's English, and the chat made only a minor difference in their conversation, made it so they did not find it unusual that they knew the same poem, so they did not find it unusual to be out late together in a bar, becoming friends; and they talked about the author of the poem and his time in Harar, and then they talked about Harar, not far from Alem's hometown and one of Michel's favorite places to visit. They talked about Michel's family history, his Canadian mother's death when he was not yet two and his subsequent removal by his father back to France; his communist upbringing there in a banlieue of Paris and his discomfort with certain elements of his present situation—how it had taken him years to adjust to having domestic help (a teenage girl from the provinces, following custom), and how his position on many things had been altered, in welcome but sometimes challenging ways, by his relationship with Alem. They talked about Eleanor, about the events that had led her here, about Abraham and Danny K.M. and Ross and Crescent Farm; about the months after her ousting, which she spent at her friend's house, one station-stop south of Albany, sleeping alternately in the daughter's lower bunk and on the sofa, depending on whose week it was with the kids, and—between trips to the city to put a few things in storage, return the keys to her shared office and wish Abraham, who'd returned only to leave again, bon voyage—working first at the book counter and then behind the bar at the place with the many tattooed forearms; and about how at precisely 11:24 p.m. on September the fifth she had left her thirties behind in the middle of her shift, and each of the forearms had raised its glass for a toast. And after even more chat and peanuts and beer, they talked at last and at length about the thing that had happened; and as they talked they took note of the particular pleasure of talking, and as they talked about the pleasure of talking they laughed, and he may or may not have understood everything she said, and she may or may not have understood everything he said, and when there finally was a pause in the conversation they smiled shyly at each other, pulled out their wallets, split the cost of their drugs and their beers, and stepped out into the now-bustling street.

Michel dropped Eleanor off in front of her apartment. When she told him how much she was paying for it, he said the price was too high and he and Alem could help her find something better. "Or see something of the country. There are busses, inexpensive ones. Why not go somewhere, why not to Harar?"

He gave her his home phone number and she gave him her email address and they parted, kissing twice on each cheek.

"I keep meaning to ask," he said, pressing his thumb into my kidney and swerving us away from the picture window, "what happens to Eleanor's libido? Even the Rocket seems to disappear in part three."

An ambulance followed by a fire truck barreled toward and past us; I couldn't tell if I'd missed the last beat of his thought.

"I don't know . . ."

He didn't appear to be listening to me, though there was nothing else in particular he was paying attention to.

"Maybe she's still catching up to herself," I said, removing his hand from my back and rubbing the spot where it had been. "Is it necessarily flight or sublimation to privilege, for a while anyway, alternative forms of desire?"

ELEANOR STUDIED. She read the books she had brought with her and the e-books she had downloaded impulsively to her laptop at the gate while waiting for her boarding zone to be called. Some of the books she had brought or downloaded were about Arthur.

That wasn't exactly right. It's not about being allowed on the mat. It's about having a say in what game is being played.

She studied the life of a man, a poet, attempting to put together the available facts and theories—attempting, impossibly, to distinguish theory from fact. She drank macchiatos at the outdoor tables of the octagonal café until her laptop battery ran out, and then she made small talk with the barista—her name was Genet (a hard "g") and she was a student at the art college—who after three days of this asked if Eleanor would like a tour of the museum on the university campus. Eleanor said yes and they set a date for the following week. She returned the next day to read more theories and facts about Arthur, only some of which registered on the saturated screen of her mind.

Still young, though not as young as before, having already been shot in the wrist by his lover, having already been an adulterer, a _____ and a poet, the son of a man who _____ and a woman who _____, he would have arrived on the horn of Africa in a _____.

He was by all accounts a _____ youth and would have struck the residents of that place as _____, although who exactly the residents would have been and if any came to greet him is up for question.

He loved men, but he loved women also, which made some give him the upper hand—though he denied, at least in public, being a top.

His brother, Frédéric, a bus conductor, would live into his sixties, while Arthur was destined to expire much sooner, though—thanks to the famous youthful photo of him—not as soon as is generally imagined when his name comes up. He would have been _____ when he settled in Harar, lured by the promise of _____ and _____ and a continued will, now already _____ years old, to leave poetry behind.

"Do you ever wonder," he asked, taking another drag, "what—if anything—you can do in the time you have left?"

As a child, he drove teachers mad with his scholastic success; his classmates too were agitated by his wolverine mind.

"While still a kid, he had already become resolutely antibourgeois in the great tradition of French bourgeois authors," wrote Edmund White in his book subtitled *The Double Life of a Rebel*.

"Everything useful is ugly," wrote Théophile Gautier in *Mademoiselle de Maupin*. The sentiment would have been picked up by Arthur in his youth through his interest in "art for art's sake," fueled by a bookstore near his home that stocked the *Contemporary Parnassus* review.

A young professor who tutored the even-younger Arthur, who led him to Rabelais, Villon, et al., would be blamed for the direction the poet's life took, for decades after his death.

That the ecstatic discovery of "I is an other," written in a letter by the juvenile Arthur to his tutor, is among the poet's most lasting legacies would suggest that the power of the articulation is transferable; this might in turn be said to endow it with a non-Parnassian use-value, leveraged in this formula from Richard Hell in his review of White's biography: "One witnesses one's invention by life."

At some point he would announce his devotion to "free freedom."

At some point he would write the poem "My Bohemia."

At some point he would chant "Order has been banished!" with the Communards.

At some point he would write "Merde à Dieu" on the walls of his hometown.

At some point he would commit the remainder of his life to his "soles of wind."

Genet met her at the entrance to the museum, a large neoclassical building complete with portico, friezes, and wide stone steps flanked by two golden statues of muses, each holding three lamps in the air. They spent two hours wandering through the ornate rooms filled with ancient pottery, medieval icons, and Ethiopian furniture or, in the case of Haile Selassie's bedroom (the building had been the emperor's palace before the revolution), European antiques.

Displaced from her role at the coffee shop, Genet seemed reserved, which triggered a reserve in Eleanor that made their conversation stilted at first, though she did manage to glean that Genet was a native of Addis Ababa, that she made small figurative paintings about the effect of globalized advertising on women's lives, that she lived with her parents but hoped to move out soon, and that she was distressed by the current politics and by many of the changes happening in her city. Eleanor nodded, venturing that she'd noticed it felt like a construction site, and Genet said It gets worse every day.

As they lingered among the Byzantine-era icons, Genet pointed out the signature style of the Master of Sagging Cheeks and taught Eleanor how to identify the sinners in the paintings: they were the ones whose faces were painted in profile, the ones who couldn't meet the painter's gaze.

He was leading me somewhere, walking two paces ahead—a habit I always find annoying in the men who have it, who deny without exception that it has to do with dominance or control. I was struggling with my heels and I was struggling with my role. He was silent. The wind was steady and strong. Though we couldn't see it and he hadn't mentioned our destination, I assumed the lake was near.

ESTABLISHED: Jean Nicolas Arthur Rimbaud—from "Ribaud" (Eng: "ribald"), meaning "whore"—arrived in Harar, Abyssinia (now Ethiopia) in 1880.

ESTABLISHED: Beginning at age seventeen his itinerary was, essentially, as follows: Charleville, Brussels, Douai, Charleville, Paris, Charleville, Paris, Charleville, Paris, Charleville, Paris, Arras,

Paris, Charleville, Brussels, Ostend, Dover, London, Charleville, London, Dover, Ostend, Roche, London, Brussels, Roche, Brussels, Paris, Charleville, Paris, London, Scotland, Reading, various parts of Europe, Charleville, Stuttgart, Switzerland, Milan, Marseille, Charleville, Vienna, Brussels, Sumatra, Java, Ireland, Charleville, America, Copenhagen, Stockholm, Marseille, Italy, Alexandria, Cyprus, Charleville, Cyprus, Egypt, Aden, Harar, Aden, Harar, Entotto, Harar, Marseille, Charleville, Marseille, Charleville.

CONCLUDED: Before his decisive break with Europe, his most frequent destination was his childhood home: la mère, or as he referred to her, "La Mother."

After they had visited all the rooms in the museum and identified a number of sinners—an activity that made them giggle, breaking through their mutual reserve—they walked to one of Genet's favorite outdoor cafés, where their reserve returned but to a lesser degree, and they had an enthusiastic conversation about the local art scene, and compared and contrasted the particular dysfunctions of the educational institutions to which they had both, not without ambivalence, given years of their lives. They said good-bye outside the café with waves and smiles. Genet mentioned she would be off to visit relatives in the south for a few weeks but that perhaps they could visit the new Goethe-Institut museum together when she returned. Eleanor said she might travel herself, but that she'd keep in touch: more smiles and waves, and they walked off in opposite directions.

ESTABLISHED: He was dismissive of his literary accomplishments in letters written from the Horn. His poems were "rinçures," from "rinse water" or "dregs."

REPORTED: In 1873, when his ejection from the Paris scene was complete, he returned to Charleville, built a fire, and burned his poems.

SUGGESTED: In Cypress he had killed a man in anger; soon after that he fled to Aden in what would be his final departure from the continent of Europe.

ESTABLISHED: In 1887, he argued in the *Bosphore Égyptien* for France's annexation of Djibouti. He hoped to become a journalist and travel to Zanzibar.

REFUTED: He was, in addition to a gunrunner, a trader of slaves.

ESTABLISHED: He was not opposed to slavery, though his longtime servant, Djami, was not enslaved.

ESTABLISHED: He was gifted with languages and learned—besides Arabic and Amharic—both Harari and Oromo; in traditional garb, he could, eventually, pass.

CONTESTED: His rape by French soldiers in the aftermath of the Commune was the catalyst for all his decisions to come.

ESTABLISHED: In the single book he saw published in his lifetime, which he later renounced, he wrote that one must be "thoroughly modern."

PROPOSED: "He attains," writes biographer Charles Nicholl, "at the end of his long journey, a kind of luminous ordinariness."

ESTABLISHED: When he parted from Djami for good, both men openly wept.

At the end, he had lost a leg to infection.
   At the end, there was no love between him and "La Mother."
   At the end, his arms were paralyzed; only a morphine drip could soothe him.
   At the end, there was Isabelle, the beloved sister.
   "I'm going under the earth and you will walk about in the sun."

"Allah," he said.
   "Djami," he said.

His last letter, dictated to Isabelle and addressed to an imagined captain in the Messageries Maritimes, read: "Kindly inform me when I will be taken aboard the ship."

"Djami," he said.
   "Allah."

He was buried in Charleville, to which he always returned.

"THERE," HE SAID, dropping cross-legged to the sand. The beach was empty; the skies threatened rain. He scooped up a handful and let it sift onto his knee.

"I'm aware of how pathetic I must seem," he said. I was still standing, my bare feet sunk into the sand, heels in hand. The beige grains continued to fall on his dark suit pants.

"Otis Redding crashed in this lake at the height of his career. A small plane, bad weather . . . That was that. I always thought it was this lake, I figured this lake was cursed. But I looked it up recently, on Wikipedia. It wasn't this lake. It was the other lake. He died in the other lake."

"But thank you for being here," he said, keeping his eyes on the shore. "I needed you to say yes, and you did."

He thanked me often, and it wasn't always clear what the thanking was for. He once said he found it soothing to be in my debt, to be in somebody else's debt.

I placed my hand on his head.

"You never told me about the girls, that day you threw the rock. You said it was another story."

He smiled, intoned "Li-zétte Ta-ni-ká-wa" but nothing more.

I watched him drop handful after handful of sand on his knee—
a disorganized criminal meets geological time. I thought about his
film and the things it didn't address: the accented child, his origin, his accident, its aftermath. I wanted to give him something.
Permission, maybe, though it wasn't mine to give.

"It wasn't a rape," I said after a long silence, and then I thought
about his mother.

"I mean Eleanor—she wasn't raped. When will that not be the
first thing to come to mind?"

He turned to me then. My feet went numb in the cold sand.

SHE WAS GREETED at the bus station by Alem's niece, Hanna. They had no language in common, but they did what they could.

Hanna: [Something in Amharic]

Eleanor: [Grinning]

Pause.

Eleanor: [Something in English]

Hanna: [Nodding. Pointing.]

Hanna: [Something in Amharic; gesture for driving a car; gesture for a hand going around a clock.]

Eleanor: [Shaking head. Hands palm-up, gesture for I don't understand.]

Hanna: [Gesture for Follow me]

Harar was a small city but the level of activity was high. They faced a stream of pedestrians, donkeys, and cars—which here, in contrast to Addis, were all vintage French: Mercedes and Peugeots from the

'60s that she would later learn were decommissioned cabs shipped over from Europe. Women in orange-and-purple tunics walked single file along the street's edge, balancing straw baskets and jugs on their heads; men crouched on narrow sidewalks in circles of five or ten, playing games or trading unidentifiable goods. The sounds of hawkers, car horns, and music from storefronts collided, producing an enveloping force that pushed Eleanor forward, like a tailwind.

Hanna looked back to make sure her charge was keeping up, grinned when she saw that she was, and pointed to a building on the corner up ahead.

Eleanor Roosevelt, first lady and lesbian; and Eleanor of Aquitaine, divorcée, falsely accused of sterility, mother of not one but two English kings.

No longer a popular name, it derives—according to some— from Latin for "compassion" or "shining light." And to others: from Greek for "foreign" or "not the same."

"So are you going to tell me the whole story, or whether the story is true?"

THE HOTEL APPEARED to have been built in the '50s, and the interior had a feeling familiar to Eleanor from places she hadn't been to or thought of in years: Texas; California. Hanna led her up to the fourth floor and opened door number 5: brightly lit, small, with a balcony overlooking the intersection. In the relative quiet, their lack of a common language filled the room.

As Eleanor dropped her bag on the floor, opened the sliding door, and took in the view from the balcony—a patchwork of low tin-roofed structures not unlike the bars on Chechenya Street, presided over by a large, faded COCA-COLA sign (this time written in English)—Hanna pulled out a cell phone and spoke rapidly into it. When she was done she tapped Eleanor on the shoulder, then looked into her eyes and pointed to her own watch-free wrist; she held out three fingers and jabbed the index finger of her other hand toward the carpet in a motion Eleanor took to mean "downstairs." Then Hanna repeated the gesture of driving a car, then made the gesture for eating.

Eleanor believed she understood that Hanna would return later with a car and that they'd go to dinner. She nodded and grinned and nodded again. She made the gesture for In that case, maybe I'll take a nap. The bus ride had been long and she had spent much of it talking to her seatmate, an engineering student on his way to visit his grandparents in their village, where he was trying to help get a hydroelectric project off the ground. "Oromo engineering," he said, interrupting himself to point out a row of thatched-roof round dwellings by the side of the road as the bus passed by.

If she had understood Hanna correctly, she could assume her immediate future was secure, while her nonimmediate future was almost completely unknown; these combined facts, along with the pattern cast by the sun through the open-weave curtains, made Eleanor smile. Then she frowned: She had forgotten to ask Hanna (though how she would have asked this using gestures she didn't know) which time-telling system she was using when setting their date. When Hanna had held up three fingers, Eleanor assumed that—because they were now in the provinces? Or because Hanna didn't speak any European languages?—this meant 3:00 by the ancient clock, which (she had learned through a series of confusing interactions followed by the relief of Alem's explanation at the restaurant) ran six hours ahead of conventional Western time. This would put their meeting at 9:00 that evening, a reasonable time to eat. It was 5:15. Surely this was the plan Hanna meant to make.

But what if Eleanor was wrong in her assumptions about the provinces; or what if Hanna was, out of consideration for her guest, switching codes? She might not show up until 3:00 the next day, for a late lunch, which would leave Eleanor on her own for the evening. This concern dented but did not destroy Eleanor's good mood—and it was somewhat balanced out by a separate worry that, if they were to dine together that evening, the two women would exhaust their repertoire of gestures before their meals arrived.

Her worries vanished into sleep. When she woke it was 8:55. She stepped onto the balcony and looked down: Hanna in front of a mustard-yellow Peugeot, smiling broadly and waving both her hands.

"Look, there's only one real subject: the relation of being to time."

"You mean beings," I corrected.

"What?"

"The relation of beings to time."

The driver of the taxi spoke English. He explained to Eleanor that he was Hanna's brother-in-law, that he owned the car and drove it part-time as a taxi but that, really, he was a student of business at the university in nearby Dire Dawa. He explained that his wife— Hanna's sister—was home with their new baby, but he and Hanna would be showing Eleanor the town that night. He said, "Leave it to me."

Eleanor was grateful for the brother-in-law's knowledge of English, grateful for being inside his car and for the exhortation to leave it to him. As they drove through the gate in the high stone walls that surrounded the old city, and then as they mounted a twisting road to the top of a hill, Eleanor made use of the brother-in-law's abilities as an interpreter to have a polite conversation with Hanna, in which she mostly thanked her repeatedly for her hospitality and help.

In the middle of the back seat, next to Eleanor, sat a large quantity of chat wrapped loosely in a clear plastic bag. The brother-in-law laughed: "You don't know about Harar, the chat capital of the world! Anywhere else you don't chew before evening. Here, as long as it's after noon, everyone chews." Eleanor recalled the circles of crouching men from earlier in the day. "Pass it up," said the brother-in-law, and Eleanor did, taking none, this time, for herself.

At the top of the hill was a double row of cars parked near a compound consisting of an old windowed warehouse and an adjacent one-story stucco building, both well kept and lit from the exterior. An animated foursome was entering the building; Eleanor and her party followed.

Inside was a vast room lined with long communal tables at which large and small groups of people of varying ages drank pitchers of beer and ate from shared platters of fragrant food; another version of the music Eleanor heard everywhere filled whatever part of the air wasn't already full with conversation.

While downloading e-books at the airport she'd also BitTorrented the 2-D version of the new 3-D film by Jean-Luc Godard, *Goodbye to Language*.

Among the fragments, a repeated refrain: "Monsieur, est-ce qu'il est possible de construire un concept d'Afrique?"

A woman entered just as I was emerging from the stall. "I'm an old friend of one of the honorees," she volunteered, leaning over the bank of sinks to arrange her hair. "But I can't decide if I want to go talk to him or not."

"I've been there," I said, smiling at her reflection and looking for a way to dry my hands.

Eleanor, Hanna, and Hanna's brother-in-law drank from pitchers of beer and ate from platters of fragrant food and talked, the brother-in-law interpreting for the two women but never without editorializing, so that by the end of their meal Eleanor had been treated less to any deep understanding of Hanna's life and character than to the complete worldview of the aspiring entrepreneur. He would make vast sums of money and travel the world. He would own apartments in New York and Tokyo, to start. He'd been saving the proceeds from driving the taxi for a number of years, and if all went as planned he'd be leaving as early as May.

It struck Eleanor that the brother-in-law did not mention his wife and baby daughter, that his plans were built on a jet-setting lifestyle that Eleanor assumed—perhaps wrongly, she acknowledged to herself—would be challenging with an infant in tow. As additional pitchers of beer were emptied and more chat chewed—though not by Eleanor, whose appetite for intoxication had dimmed after her series of indulgences, beginning with the pot-butter kale and ending with her night out with Michel—it struck her that if she were to trust her ability to read people at all, if she knew anything about the performance of seduction and the aura of illicit love, she would suspect that these two, Hanna and her brother-in-law, were the real couple of his imagined future. Their chemistry—a word Eleanor disliked using in this way, but she was linguistically tired from the evening so far—hit Eleanor at a point on the side of her neck near her collarbone. She rubbed the spot with her hand, pretending to scratch an itch.

There was talk of dancing. They climbed into the Peugeot, which was parked pointing down the hill toward the walled city below, a security measure Eleanor understood when after a few tries the car failed to start. The brother-in-law ordered Eleanor and Hanna to stay in their seats and shifted the car into neutral, pawing at the pavement with his left foot. They glided down the hill in this manner until he pulled into a conveniently located gas station where, with some help from Hanna and the station attendant, he concocted a paste from chewing gum, water, and tissue, and used it to plug a hole somewhere in the abdomen of the car.

Without much of a choice, Eleanor agreed to whatever plans were proposed for the remainder of the evening: the raucous drive through the interior of the walled city, preceded by the obligatory stop at the gates to be photographed feeding the hyenas—a tourist trap Hanna insisted Eleanor experience—and followed by several more hours at a small club where Hanna and her brother-in-law lost their discretion and made out deliriously in plain sight. Eleanor sat alone, drinking a beer and rubbing her neck. Watching people dance reminded her of the picture of Danny K.M. she'd found on the kizomba website, the grainy printout of which she removed now from her wallet. She could hardly distinguish his face in the dark club. She smiled at Danny K.M., then placed him on the table beside her drink. At irregular intervals, possibly keyed to changes in the music too subtle for Eleanor to recognize, Hanna or her companion or one or more of the other dancers would switch into the restrained shoulder-shiver of eskista. Yewch guday new, Eleanor said softly, repeating the words Hanna had taught her in the car. Yewch guday ferengi, too, she thought. A foreigner, perhaps a barbarian.

I am—eimai—xenía, she interpreted for nobody but herself.

When an argument broke out between two of the club's patrons, Hanna grinned and made the gesture for Let's get out of here, and they ran for the car. And when Eleanor looked around and thought she understood that she was just a few long blocks from her hotel, and when she sought and gained confirmation from the brother-in-law that this was the case, she decided not to get back into the Peugeot, whose ignition might or might not turn over anyway.

She felt in this decision the echo of other decisions, of all the central and marginal decisions that, in their determining powers over the course of a life, form much of the content that replaces empty time; and she knew that the effects of the decision were consequential, even if minor, even if still unknown; and she watched the swaying couple and hoped for nothing more for them than that the car would or would not start according to their desire; and she looked up and saw the moon—just shy of perfection—and heard

herself announce, though she couldn't be sure the words were coming from her mouth, that she would walk home, which she did after
a last round of gestures and grins.

He had handed me the diploma when he came offstage and asked if
I could carry it in my bag, and now its presence there annoyed me
as I felt around, at his request, for a pen. I gave him the bag—"You
do it"—and walked away.

Lizette Tanikawa stood alone by the drinks table. I hadn't known
it was her in the bathroom before, but when I saw his face as he recognized her across the room, I guessed. I walked over to the bar,
ordered a club soda with bitters, and hovered by her side.

He was chatting with a few admirers, presumably faculty or
grad students in film, signing the occasional book. Above his head
on the wood-paneled walls hung a muted tapestry—beige, ecru, and
taupe—the central image of which was a man with an elephant's
trunk in place of a nose. Above the image was an embroidered banner spelling out the word "Africa."

"Weird tapestry," I said.

"Don't I know it," she replied, gesturing across the room to a
similar one bearing an image of a dragon-headed woman and, in
even larger letters, "Asia."

As she walked to the hotel, she thought of Arthur and the probability he had—maybe routinely—passed the same way. She thought
of the crouching men from earlier in the afternoon, and of the
Degas drawing she'd seen at the Met—*fatigue, stability, submission*—
and then she thought of her tarot deck's illustration for The Star:

a sturdy female figure, naked, with yellow hair and tan skin, bent at the knee and gazing down into a pool of water, a pitcher in each hand. With one, she fills up the pool itself; the other she empties on the bank, releasing rivulets that spill to the margins of the card. In the distance is a mountain dwarfed by the woman, the water, the banks, and—in a plane that's neither foreground nor background— all eight iterations of the illustrated star itself.

A kind of luminous ordinariness. Or another revision, a sweep— to fix errors and identify signs of excess, signs of confusion or desire.

"It's strange to teach in your hometown," she said, nodding back to a passing student.

"What department are you in?"

"Art History. And just History." The bartender refilled her wine.

The next morning she found, in her jacket's inner pocket, the corner she had ripped from the page before throwing it in the fire. She swallowed it. It wasn't like her to do this. But what was Eleanor like?

"I'm writing an article," she said, "on *The Progress of Love*. Do you know it?" I laughed. "If only!" An image of Kat the previous morning leaving for good, bags in hand. Sweet smile and eyes flashing into the future.

And what does it mean to ask what she was like?

"The sequence of paintings by Fragonard. I'm fascinated not only by their eroticism but by their trajectory—their commission, their completion in the wake of the revolution, their installation in the Château du Barry and subsequent rejection and removal. The fickleness of the patron is interesting, but my book isn't about any of that. It's about the role of the written word in the paintings. So"— she lowered her voice and leaned in—"there's the one-handed book the girl reads in *The Lover Crowned,* which was painted after the rejection and which, to my mind, is the most erotic moment in the narrative, and then in the original set that final, platonic rereading of the love letters: completely tame! The Platonism in general could fill a book—God, I'm sorry, I slipped into lecture mode. I just taught this stuff all week."

Before I had the chance to respond, her attention went elsewhere: "Oh look," she said, "I guess he's decided to come say hello."

Aidan was walking toward us. He looked unsteady but firm, though not firm enough to deflect the pleasantries of another admirer, this one in catering uniform carrying an empty drinks tray.

She spent an afternoon with her notebook, barely leaving her bed. The sentences and paragraphs found her, then arranged themselves of their own accord, the way sleep had a way, though less so of late—as if the quantity of new information she absorbed each day required a deeper nightly evacuation—of rearranging her mind. Later, she read the entirety of what she had written out loud to herself, marking the gaps in her text with the gesture for More content shall be inserted here once that content is both knowable and known.

The thinking reflected in the writing was both familiar and not, both reminded her of the site of her lost paragraphs and felt clearly like a new and unfamiliar field on which she had been invited, or invited herself, to play. At times during the writing she felt nervous, shameful, or exposed—especially when it seemed to reflect equally her ignorance and her curiosity about her surroundings—and she did her best to fold her nerves, shame, and exposure into the text itself, without relying on this tactic to provide a solution to her discomfort. The way the paragraphs arranged themselves was as an abecedary, a collection of sentences sorted by the English alphabet, which she had been staring at for days on a printed study sheet she'd found in the hotel-room desk, its twenty-six letters keyed more or less to the Amharic letters she was trying to learn.

Before setting down the notebook, she pronounced the titles of the paragraphs again:

A: Addis
B: Bananas
C: Carbon
D: Danny K.M.
E: English
F: Ferengi
G: Goethe
H: Hagiography
I: Italy
J: Jazz
K: Kettle of Fish
L: Lucy
M: Marathon
N:
O:
P: Prayer

Q: Quat (chat)
R:
S: Sex Work
T: Teff
U: Untranslatability
V:
W:
X: Xenía
Z: Zoo

and then she took a nap.

"Well," Lizette continued, her eyes having dimmed, "I suppose also"—she brought her right hand to her lips and let out a short sigh through her nose, like a horse, then shook her head—"I am fascinated by what follows a major rejection. This one"—she waved her free hand toward Aidan, who had been intercepted once again, this time by the dean of Humanities, the convocation's host—"I was supposed to marry. We were going to have three children and live in Spain, or was it Corsica. But before that could become more than just talk, he retreated"—she paused almost imperceptibly—"there was a horrible accident, and one of our classmates was injured as a result. Then my future husband and his family were gone. And the other one, Miranda"—she nodded toward the dean—"gave me a shoulder to cry on. You know the word *rejection*"—she paused, lips pursed—"once meant, or also meant, to throw something back, to return it to the field of play. Anyway. Miranda and I were friends for a decade before we got it together to fuck, but we never really attached to anyone else. We tried for years to have kids. We both tried, we had four miscarriages between us. And now we have two we adopted through the foster system. They're brothers, eight and ten now. It's funny: the way we look, and the way our kids look, if we were a straight couple we'd pass for a bio family. They were out of diapers when the dean's job opened up, and the day she got it, I found out I'd been approved for tenure. It's a miracle it all worked out so well."

Now he had a clear path in our direction.

"I'd like to say I can't imagine my life going a different way. But to be honest,"—she turned to look at me—"I can. Can't you?"

THE WOMAN CALLED ELEANOR emerges from her hotel wearing a taupe dress, canvas sneakers, a light sweater, and white plastic-rim sunglasses. The sun is strong. She squints up at the sky, smiles.

An hour later she is intercepted by a professional guide at the southern entrance to the old town. They greet each other, walk together through the gate.

An hour later, the woman and the guide have completed the loop, which ends at the flesh market in the central square. He points to the carcasses of goats with curled horns and to a severed camel's head. "Go on, take a picture," he urges. She tells him she can't; she has forgotten to charge her phone.

Seventeen minutes later, the guide and the woman sit drinking macchiatos at the counter of a small café. The woman asks to be shown Bet Rimbo. He gestures down a narrow street and says But it's Tuesday; on Tuesdays the Rimbaud House is closed.

Twenty minutes later they're circling the walls of the city in an open-top jeep. The guide narrates the past; the woman asks questions. Again he encourages her to take pictures, again she demurs.

Eighteen minutes before their time together is up, the woman thanks the guide, hands him some bills, smiles, and walks away.

She can be seen removing her sunglasses and approaching a large Victorian house. She walks around the house, which is painted turquoise and yellow, and sits on the stoop. A careful observer would note a peculiar brightness in the air immediately surrounding the woman, as if the wattage within a certain radius of her body had increased.

Time passes. The woman rises and walks into a nearby restaurant where she eats alone, her sunglasses perched on top of her head.

At one point she leans her elbows on the table and places her chin in her hands.

At one point she cocks her head to the right as if recalling something pleasant.

At one point she takes a sharp breath as if recalling something painful.

The next morning the woman, in the same dress and same canvas sneakers, with the same peculiar brightness in her margins, enters through the east gate to the city and sits down in an internet café.

Don't forget Eleanor in "Ease Down the Road," its defense of fugitive desire between friends.

There were 137 messages in her priority in-box. Among them were notes from her friends, including one from a poet she hadn't heard from in years asking for Eleanor's current address so she could send a copy of her latest handmade book. There were several updates from Abraham, the last of which showed him beginning to worry at her silence. There was a message from Dawit, who was eager to meet her. And there was an update from Ross, to which he'd attached a picture of himself sitting at one of the Formica tables at the Muddy Cup, shoulder to shoulder with a smiling woman whose silver hair was streaked with a becoming mauve.

Despite her distance from news of it, the stream of events flowed on. The White House, in what some deemed a late-term legacy move, had announced an opening of relations with Cuba. The grand jury verdict was just days away; Ferguson and the world stood by. Some documentary filmmakers were being accused of treason, and just that morning more than five thousand acres of California desert had been burned in a fire. She stopped the stream temporarily, closing the window. She got up.

Lizette and I took turns swapping his whiskey for water. He thanked us each time, then went back to the bar for another.

In two days she had moved to an extended-stay room in the hotel, equipped with a kitchenette.

In four days she had bought a prepaid phone from which she could send international texts.

In seven days, thanks to a series of small coincidences and her language skills, she had landed an unofficial job at the Rimbaud House, filling in for an assistant who had just given birth. She was trained quickly to clean and maintain the exhibits and give occasional tours in English and in broken French.

She met a woman named Maaza, who had grown up in Addis and Harar but studied at UCLA and was writing a thesis about the effect of the country's new tribal identification mandate on community ties. Maaza was staying with her brother, Tadese, an organizer in the struggling national labor movement, whom Eleanor liked talking with and who seemed to find her amusing—which at first she took to mean that he found her ridiculous. The day after they met, Tadese took her on a tour of Harar that was geographically similar to the one led by the professional guide (a friend of Hanna's brother-in-law, whose offer of an introduction she hadn't wanted to refuse). In place of the guide's enthusiastic but canned patter and prescribed photo ops, Tadese offered a running history lesson, grounding each site in contextualizing facts—about the class politics of agricultural land use and labor, about the structures of power and resistance during the Italian years, the Derg years, and more recent years—in a sense embodying the things Eleanor had been reading about in books with a clarity and generosity that she took note of, both to herself and, shyly over lunch, to Tadese himself.

"I can't explain why. I've always told the wrong secrets to the wrong people for the wrong reasons. Also, my lie to you was closer to truth than when I tell the truth."

On the eighth day she texted a picture to Abraham of a touring motorcycle—a BMW RT1100, with metal side panniers—parked on the corner of her street.

One afternoon at work she received an envelope in the mail: the chapbook, slim and bound by hand with waxed thread, from her old poet-friend. Its title was *Robot Hug from Behind*, and the poems it contained were about friendship, or they were about class and race and the prison-industrial complex, or about technology and authenticity, or they were about the news.

"The opposite of suicide / is learning and creating with friends / the necessary social tries to trick us," she read, sitting on the warm steps of Bet Rimbo, her sunglasses on.

She kept reading until she finished. She had the thought or the feeling that she was all-in with these poems, and took note. She had the feeling or the thought that this book was sent from her future: six blank pages at its end.

After two weeks had passed, she bought paper and envelopes.

To the friend whose comforter she had stained with the blood from her thumb she wrote _____.

To the friend who had let her sleep in her daughter's bunk bed she wrote _____.

To Alem and Michel she wrote: Rendez-moi visite! Vous me manquez!

To Ross she wrote a long letter about the holdings of the museum, quoting portions of Arthur's correspondence that were exhibited in the vitrines.

To her poet-friend she sent a sun-faded notebook she'd bought on the street and a handwritten copy of three of her paragraphs, signed with a heart.

To Crescent Farm she sent the Polaroid of herself feeding the hyenas. On the back she printed in capital letters: WE ARE PERFORMANCE THAT IS QUALITY LIFE TRY NOW.

She didn't have Genet's postal address so she texted her instead: "I'll be in Harar for at least the next six weeks. I'm sorry to miss the Goethe-Institut, but I hope we can still go before my visa and my Visa run out. Until then, amasaganalo for the hospitality and all the delicious bunna!" After some thought, she signed her text: "Warmly, Eleanor."

We cabbed home from the airport and he dropped me off. We each looked out our separate windows as the lights streaked by. He promised to send me *The Fourth Flight* in installments—it would read best that way; he didn't want me flipping around. He closed his eyes and I thought he'd fallen asleep until he spoke: "Footless tights. You always left early. I figured you had to get to a dance class or something, so I didn't mind." I opened my mouth to speak, though I didn't know what I would say, but he went on: "Also. Also—I like what you did with your title. Though you didn't use my favorite. My favorite was *She Got Up*."

For the last five minutes of the ride we touched each other's hands.

THE NEXT MORNING she'll stop at the café on her way to work. She'll read about a boat carrying several hundred refugees that has capsized outside Lampedusa, close enough to shore that the cries of the drowning were audible from land. She'll read that the death toll of the migrants, most of them from Somalia and Eritrea, is rising into the hundreds. She won't read about the rapes these same migrants endured before dying so close to their destination because these facts won't emerge for weeks or months, and the delay of these facts will be merciful because Eleanor's stores of tolerance for the stream of intolerable events has shrunk. She will not cry for the refugees—her temporary neighbors—because the feeling produced by their fate will not be one of melancholia, though what it will be won't be easy to name; and she will read instead another item about the death from illness, days after his release from decades in prison, of a member of the Angola Three, and her response to this too will be subtly different from what she knew. She will note the difference, which she'll carry with her through her day at Bet Rimbo, through her solitary walk home via the flesh market, the spice market, and the chat market; she'll find herself periodically throughout the day succumbing to a sensation of being broken apart like a wishbone, followed immediately by a sensation of sliding on a freshly polished concrete floor, and she'll note the strange juxtaposition of these images and their lack of attachment to any direct memory or experience, and she'll note the discomfort and pleasure attending this lack; and when she arrives at her building and exchanges nods with her downstairs neighbor and climbs up the three flights of stairs, she'll open the door to an ordinary room containing an ordinary table and bed and an ordinary stove, and she'll walk to the stove and light it with a match to bring a luminously ordinary pot of water to life.

Later, she'll walk up the hill to the brewery for shiro and beers with Maaza and Tadese.

THE DAY AFTER the ceremony we had the morning free—our flight didn't leave until five-thirty. After breakfast, we'd decided to take a walk through campus. Outside the art museum, a massive brutalist structure amid the friendly brick, a small sign read: Alfred Leslie's *The Killing Cycle*.

Six canvases and three watercolors occupied the main gallery. Aidan sat before one of the paintings and didn't move for an hour. I looked at them all and then went into the adjacent room, where the cinematic collaboration between Leslie and Frank O'Hara, *The Last Clean Shirt*, was being projected in a loop. In it, a black man drives a white woman around the East Village in a convertible. It's 1964. They are young, fashionable, full of life. The man has taped a clock to the dashboard; the film is a single take, seven minutes long. The man remains silent—though expressive in his gestures—while the woman keeps up an incomprehensible monologue of what the wall text calls "Finnish gibberish." She pauses once to light a cigarette and twice more in moments of apparent self-consciousness, when a cloud passes over her otherwise carefree face. The film is composed of three iterations of the same take: one with no subtitles, one with subtitles ostensibly translating the woman's speech, one in which the subtitles seem to express the thoughts of the silent man.

"It's in the nature of all of us to want to be unconnected," she says. "To want to be unconnected / And you should pull us all together / like Humpty Dumpty / or something."

"I could do this a lot easier with chewing gum," he thinks, taping the clock once more to the dash.

"I really am upset about things," she says. "I mean it's a rotten life / Everything that goes on around you is ridiculous."

When I emerged from the darkened room he was still there, seated on the tufted bench, alone with *The Cocktail Party.* According to the catalog, this was one of the paintings Leslie had edited out of his famous sequence depicting O'Hara's death, at forty, on the beach at Fire Island. Now the painter had allowed the gallery to reassemble all of the extant canvasses—six, to the three of his edited version— and had added subtitles beneath two of them. The hand-lettered text that now captioned *The Cocktail Party* was taken from O'Hara's script for *The Last Clean Shirt,* a quote from the woman's monologue that I spent some time trying to parse before giving up:

I have the other idea about guilt. It's not in us, it's in the situation. You don't say that the victim is responsible for a concentration camp or a Mack truck.

I have typed, by mistake, more than once here, "Frank O'Harar."

The painting is rectangular, landscape view. The left third is occupied by two figures in bathing suits, both slim, both tall, with tanned white skin. They are looking down on the beach from a balcony or ledge. Her back is to us, her hands clasped behind red-and-white-striped bikini bottoms. He, at her side, is half turned to the right, cocktail in hand. They seem to overlap rather than touch, as if they are together in the space of the painting but not in the space of the world. They're lit from behind—which means we too are lit from behind—by an electric light or the moon, we can't know which. In the foreground, on a small table next to the man's hip, are a plate of potato chips and Oreos, a rotary phone with a white business card beside it, a flowered mug, two lemon wedges, and a small brown dome that might be a chocolate truffle or macaroon. We see his face in profile; he is lost in thought, maybe gazing at the last traces of twilight on the cove. On the beach below: two vehicles, the glow of headlights, an illegible but ominous scene. Perhaps there is far-away yelling: A poet has been killed while sleeping on the beach. An accident. Any thing may produce any thing.

Aidan was doing the thing with his fingers again: pinky, ring, middle, index, thumb. His lips had settled into a faraway smile, and I watched him not weep while clearly weeping in his mind. He'd never reminded me so much of Eleanor.

The sounds of honking and traffic and the woman's shrill speech filtered in from the other room. I looked from the painting to my friend and back again.

The phone on the table is black. The glow from the headlights is yellow. The cocktail is red.

It's night, but the sky is blue. A variegated blue.

ACKNOWLEDGMENTS

Thanks to all of the writers and artists who are mentioned or quoted in this book; to Matthew Akers and Jeff Dupre for their film *Marina Abramović: The Artist Is Present;* and to the curators of the 2014 exhibition *Alfred Leslie: The Killing Cycle* at the Haggerty Museum of Art in Milwaukee. Facts and propositions about Rimbaud's later years are drawn mostly from Charles Nicholl's book *Somebody Else: Arthur Rimbaud in Africa.* Thanks to Jacqueline Waters for publishing *She Got Up*—this novel's prototext—as a pamphlet from The Physiocrats in 2012, to Damon Krukowski and Naomi Yang for publishing an early excerpt on their *Exact Change* app, and to all three for their friendship and examples as artist-publishers.

Significant work was made possible—and pleasurable—by two residencies at Writers OMI and one at Headlands Center for the Arts. Thanks to DW Gibson, Sean Uyehara, Holly Blake, my fellow residents, and the wonderful staff of both. I am grateful to Steven Rand and apexart for facilitating the outbound residency program that brought me to Ethiopia in 2009, and to Siri Hustvedt for nominating me. Following the intent of that program, I formed no expectations about producing work related to my experience, and only years later did fragments of it become reference points for Eleanor's story. I offer my affectionate gratitude to Konjit Seyoum and her family, Mihret Kebede, Azeb

Worku and her family, Emma Lochery, Surafel Wondimu, the late Michael Daniel Ambachew, Asni arts, NETSA arts village, the Goethe-Institut Äthiopien, and the many artists, scholars, neighbors, and others who welcomed me and shared their knowlege and experience during my stay and after.

Thanks to Amanda Annis for stalwart guidance, generosity, and friendship; to Erika Stevens, Carla Valadez, Mandy Medley, Caroline Casey, Chris Fischbach, Carlos Esparza, and everyone at Coffee House Press; and to Rose-Lynn Fisher for the cover image and the story behind it. Thanks to markbvt at advrider.com for the lingo.

Warm thanks to my friends and fellow writers who offered feedback, insight, and support, including Jarrod Annis, Mirene Arsanios, David Buuck, Amina Cain, Kelli Cain, Corina Copp, Ellie Ga, Renee Gladman, Jane Gregory, Jennifer Kabat, Jonathan Lethem, Ben Lerner, Sarah McCarry, Maaza Mengiste, Maggie Nelson, rectangle, Nelly Reifler, Sarah Riggs, DglsN.Rthsjchld, Shelby Shaw, Anna Stein, Simone White, Rebecca Wolff, and Matvei Yankelevich; to Rachel Wasserman; to Lara Durback for writing *Robot Hug From Behind* and sending it to me just in time; to Joan, Yiannis, and Nick Moschovakis; to Trevor Wilson; and to Carin Besser, without whose encouragement and labor this book would not have found its shape, and without whose lifelong friendship and dialogue I could not have begun to find mine. This is dedicated to her.

Coffee House Press began as a small letterpress operation in 1972 and has grown into an internationally renowned nonprofit publisher of literary fiction, essay, poetry, and other work that doesn't fit neatly into genre categories.

Coffee House is both a publisher and an arts organization. Through our *Books in Action* program and publications, we've become interdisciplinary collaborators and incubators for new work and audience experiences. Our vision for the future is one where a publisher is a catalyst and connector.

LITERATURE
is not the same thing as
PUBLISHING

FUNDER ACKNOWLEDGMENTS

Coffee House Press is an internationally renowned independent book publisher and arts nonprofit based in Minneapolis, MN; through its literary publications and *Books in Action* program, Coffee House acts as a catalyst and connector—between authors and readers, ideas and resources, creativity and community, inspiration and action.

Coffee House Press books are made possible through the generous support of grants and donations from corporations, state and federal grant programs, family foundations, and the many individuals who believe in the transformational power of literature. This activity is made possible by the voters of Minnesota through a Minnesota State Arts Board Operating Support grant, thanks to the legislative appropriation from the arts and cultural heritage fund. Coffee House also receives major operating support from the Amazon Literary Partnership, the Jerome Foundation, The McKnight Foundation, Target Foundation, and the National Endowment for the Arts (NEA). To find out more about how NEA grants impact individuals and communities, visit www.arts.gov.

Coffee House Press receives additional support from the Elmer L. & Eleanor J. Andersen Foundation; the David & Mary Anderson Family Foundation; Bookmobile; the Buuck Family Foundation; Fredrikson & Byron, P.A.; Dorsey & Whitney LLP; the Fringe Foundation; Kenneth Koch Literary Estate; the Knight Foundation; the Matching Grant Program Fund of the Minneapolis Foundation; Mr. Pancks' Fund in memory of Graham Kimpton; the Schwab Charitable Fund; Schwegman, Lundberg & Woessner, P.A.; the U.S. Bank Foundation; and VSA Minnesota for the Metropolitan Regional Arts Council.

THE PUBLISHER'S CIRCLE OF COFFEE HOUSE PRESS

Publisher's Circle members make significant contributions to Coffee House Press's annual giving campaign. Understanding that a strong financial base is necessary for the press to meet the challenges and opportunities that arise each year, this group plays a crucial part in the success of Coffee House's mission.

Recent Publisher's Circle members include many anonymous donors, Suzanne Allen, Patricia A. Beithon, the E. Thomas Binger & Rebecca Rand Fund of the Minneapolis Foundation, Andrew Brantingham, Robert & Gail Buuck, Claire Casey, Louise Copeland, Jane Dalrymple-Hollo, Mary Ebert & Paul Stembler, Kaywin Feldman & Jim Lutz, Chris Fischbach & Katie Dublinski, Sally French, Jocelyn Hale & Glenn Miller, the Rehael Fund-Roger Hale/Nor Hall of the Minneapolis Foundation, Randy Hartten & Ron Lotz, Dylan Hicks & Nina Hale, William Hardacker, Randall Heath, Jeffrey Hom, Carl & Heidi Horsch, Amy L. Hubbard & Geoffrey J. Kehoe Fund, Kenneth Kahn & Susan Dicker, Stephen & Isabel Keating, Kenneth Koch Literary Estate, Cinda Kornblum, Jennifer Kwon Dobbs & Stefan Liess, Lambert Family Foundation, Lenfestey Family Foundation, Sarah Lutman & Rob Rudolph, the Carol & Aaron Mack Charitable Fund of the Minneapolis Foundation, George & Olga Mack, Joshua Mack & Ron Warren, Gillian McCain, Malcolm S. McDermid & Katie Windle, Mary & Malcolm McDermid, Sjur Midness & Briar Andresen, Maureen Millea Smith & Daniel Smith, Peter Nelson & Jennifer Swenson, Enrique & Jennifer Olivarez, Alan Polsky, Marc Porter & James Hennessy, Robin Preble, Alexis Scott, Ruth Stricker Dayton, Jeffrey Sugerman & Sarah Schultz, Nan G. & Stephen C. Swid, Kenneth Thorp in memory of Allan Kornblum & Rochelle Ratner, Patricia Tilton, Joanne Von Blon, Stu Wilson & Melissa Barker, Warren D. Woessner & Iris C. Freeman, Margaret Wurtele, and Wayne P. Zink & Christopher Schout.

For more information about the Publisher's Circle and other ways to support Coffee House Press books, authors, and activities, please visit www.coffeehousepress.org/support or contact us at info@coffeehousepress.org.

ANNA MOSCHOVAKIS's books include *They and We Will Get into Trouble for This, You and Three Others Are Approaching a Lake* (winner of the James Laughlin Award), and English translations of Albert Cossery's *The Jokers*, Annie Ernaux's *The Possession*, and *Bresson on Bresson*. She is a longtime member of the Brooklyn-based publishing collective Ugly Duckling Presse and cofounder of Bushel, a collectively run art and community space in the Catskills. This is her first novel.

Eleanor, or, The Rejection of the Progress of Love
was typeset by Bookmobile Design & Digital Publisher Services.
Text is set in Adobe Caslon Pro.